LADY NOGGS, PEERESS

He had them through the crowd, past the ticket-barrier,
and into a hansom in eighty seconds

LADY NOGGS, PEERESS
BY EDGAR JEPSON
Author of "The Admirable Tinker"

New York: McClure, Phillips & Co.: Mcmv

CONTENTS

CHAPTER   PAGE

   I THE LADY NOGGS APOLOGIZES . . .   3

  II THE SPOILED ADVERTISEMENT . . .   20

 III SIX RABBITS A WEEK   45

 IV THE LADY NOGGS FLAGS THE NORTH-
ERN STAR   72

  V THE LADY NOGGS RECEIVES AN IN-
VITATION   97

 VI A VARIATION IN THE ART OF POODLE-
SHAVING   111

VII THE LADY NOGGS RETURNS . . .   131

VIII THE LADY NOGGS FINDS A NEW
FRIEND   151

 IX AN UNHAPPY CONFERENCE   169

  X THE PERILS OF PHILANTHROPY. . .   185

 XI MR. BORRODAILE IS FIRM   201

 XII THE IMPOSSIBLE UNCLE   217

XIII AN INFORMAL INTRODUCTION . . .   237

XIV IN THE BRIGAND'S LAIR   252

 XV THE WEDDING GUEST   289

LIST OF ILLUSTRATIONS

He Had Them Through the Crowd, Past
the Ticket-Barrier, and Into a Hansom
in Eighty Seconds . . . . *Frontispiece*

FACING
PAGE

"Oh, Well, She's Just Explained That
She's Made Me Bald for Life" . . 18

"My Name is Lady Felicia Grandison. How
Do You Do?" and Dropped with an
Old-Fashioned Curtsey 28

"Oh, What a Wicked Child! to Play a
Trick, and Then Tell a Lie About It!" 42

She Came Out of the Building Between
Two Groups 70

The Intelligent Animals Trotted Into the
Dining-Room in a Body 128

Five Hooligans Dashed Out Upon Them . 192

"Mr. Albert, Mr. Jerry, the Duchess of
Huddersfield" 198

LADY NOGGS, PEERESS

CHAPTER ONE

THE LADY NOGGS APOLOGIZES

I'M afraid you've had a tiring evening, Mr. Borrodaile," said the Prime Minister with gentle commiseration, pausing at his bedroom door. "It was unfortunate that those despatches came so late."

"Not at all, sir; not at all," protested his secretary.

"Well, we have disposed of them, at any rate, which is always something gained," said the Prime Minister, passing his fingers combwise through his beard; and he sighed as if an infinite load of regret for "something accomplished, something done," weighed upon his scrupulous soul. "You must take a holiday to-morrow," he added. "Good-night."

"Thank you, sir; good-night," said his secretary, and went along the corridor to his bedroom.

The Prime Minister sighed again; opened his

bedroom door, and switched on the electric light. He stopped to sigh again before shutting the door; and from his secretary's room, at the end of the corridor, there came a clattering crash, a swish of falling water, and a loud swear-word.

The Prime Minister rushed out of his bedroom, down the corridor, to the scene of the crash, and found himself gazing over a broken water-jug at Mr. Borrodaile, who stood in the middle of his room, dripping from head to foot, and rubbing viciously his sopping head, with a very rueful face.

"Whatever has happened?" cried the startled Prime Minister.

"Booby-trap," said his secretary, curtly.

"Dear, dear! this is very distressing!" said the Prime Minister. "I'm afraid it must have been Lady Felicia."

"Little fiend!" muttered the secretary, rubbing still. A water-jug, loaded with its proper element, will raise a bump on the hardest head; and Mr. Borrodaile had the thin skull of a clever man.

"I'm very sorry," said the Prime Minister. "I will speak to her about it. I must really be very severe with her."

His secretary grinned through his ruefulness, as if he pictured the scene, and saw his chief engaged in the heroic effort. "Please don't trouble about it, sir," he said. "It really doesn't matter. But I should like to know," he added thoughtfully, "what I've done to offend her."

"But I *shall* trouble about it," said the Prime Minister, firmly. "It is in the highest degree unreasonable that a little girl should take offence at the doings of her elders, and play these tricks on them. I shall be very severe with her — very. Is there anything I can do for you?"

"No, thank you; no, thank you. It's really nothing at all. Merely a matter of having my clothes dried to-morrow. Please don't let me keep you up; you are tired out, working at those despatches."

"Well, if you're sure I can do nothing. But, believe me, I regret this occurrence very much. Good-night."

"Good-night, sir. Please don't let it trouble you."

But it did trouble the Prime Minister. It seemed to him hard that the Emperor Fritz and the Lady Felicia Grandison should have seen fit to behave badly on the same evening; though, to his credit be it said, the bad behaviour of the Emperor Fritz, to which he was used, troubled him very much less than the bad behaviour of the Lady Felicia, to which he was also used.

He lay awake sighing and debating, with very much less skill than he was wont to display in Parliament, whether he had really done wisely in taking his dead sister's child to live with him, whether he was quite the man to superintend the up-bringing of a little girl. His theory of the subject was, he knew, excellent; but he found that practice so seldom squared with it.

He fell from his troubled debate into no less troubled dreams, in which he dodged showers of exceedingly vicious water-jugs falling from a serene sky.

He dressed next morning in no little trepidation, for he had bound himself to speak severely to the Lady Felicia, and he was very doubtful how the Lady Felicia would take it. He realized with a sigh how much sooner he would háve faced an infuriated House than his unrighteously indignant niece. He knew that she would be indignant, but he did not know what form her indignation would take; and the uncertainty added nothing to his comfort.

He was relieved, therefore, to find that she was not yet in the breakfast-room when he came down; it gave him time to take his seat at the table and compose his features to the proper judicial sternness. Then he began his breakfast. Presently he heard a scurrying of swift feet; the door burst open as though persuaded by a tornado; and the Lady Felicia entered, or rather tumbled into the room, a dazzling vision of violet velvet, flushed cheeks, flying hair, and sparkling eyes — a figure which might have stepped, or, to be exact, tumbled out of a picture by Sir Joshua Reynolds.

"Good-morning, uncle," she said. "I'm sorry to be late! And I shouldn't be if Miss Caldecott didn't make me change into a picture frock to come to breakfast in. She says that brown holland would ruffle your — your — oh, what is it ? — your artistic sensibilities."

And she came to him, and put up her face to be kissed.

"Good-morning, Felicia," said the Prime Minister bending down.

"Noggs," said the Lady Felicia curtly, removing her face out of reach.

"Felicia, I cannot—"

"Noggs! Noggs! Noggs!" cried the child. "If

you don't call me Noggs, and call me Felicia
again, I shall think you are angry with me and
cry." And she blinked her eyes with inconceiv-
able swiftness twenty or thirty times to bring
the tears into them.

The Prime Minister hesitated, and was lost;
then he said quickly but stiffly, "Noggs."

"That's right," said the Lady Felicia; she
kissed him in a perfunctory fashion, and slipped
into her chair.

"I'm exceedingly distressed by your conduct," said the Prime Minister with sufficient
severity. "Last night you set a — a booby-trap
above Mr. Borrodaile's door, and caused him
considerable pain and inconvenience."

"Billy's a pig!" cried the Lady Noggs
shortly.

The Prime Minister blinked painfully; on
the spur of the moment he could not make up
his accurate mind whether it was more of a
shock to him to hear the sedate Mr. Borrodaile
called Billy, or described as an unattractive
animal.

"That — that is not the way for a little girl
to speak of her elders," he said unhappily.

"If Billy sneaked, then he's a pig!" said the
Lady Noggs firmly.

"I can't understand how you could bring yourself to play any one such an unkind trick."

"It served him right," said the Lady Noggs.

"Served him right? How? I'm sure that Mr. Borrodaile did nothing — nothing to deserve such treatment."

"Oh, yes, he did," said the Lady Noggs, quickly. "I never tell tales — never. But he's sneaked about that booby-trap ; and I'll tell about him. What do you think he called you ?"

"I don't know, and I don't want to hear!" cried the Prime Minister quickly.

"He called you a philosopher," said the Lady Noggs with dreadful gravity. "I heard him tell Sir George that you were a philosopher."

The Prime Minister laughed gently; and then he laughed louder.

The Lady Noggs looked scandalized by his levity. "I think it's a horrid thing to be called," she said severely. "Only last Sunday Mr. Cringle said in his sermon that philosophers were very wicked men."

"I'm sorry that Mr. Cringle takes such a harsh view of them," said the Prime Minister. "But I can't help Mr. Cringle. I am a philosopher; and I don't think I'm a very wicked man."

The Lady Noggs looked horrified; then her

face cleared slowly, and she said: "Oh, no; if you're a philosopher, they're not wicked men. Mr. Cringle was wrong."

"I'm glad you look at it like that," said the Prime Minister. "And so you see you had no grievance against Mr. Borrodaile."

"Oh yes, I had," said the Lady Noggs quickly. "He'd no right to call you a philosopher."

The Prime Minister gazed at her with bewildered eyes; he could not follow her reasoning. "Well, at any rate," he said, "you must apologize to him."

"Apologize to Billy?" cried the Lady with unaffected scorn.

The Prime Minister quivered to the name Billy, but he said firmly: "Yes; I insist upon it."

The Lady Noggs considered her uncle's face carefully; seemed to weigh the matter, and made up her mind that he was in earnest. Then a curious gleam came into her eyes, and she said, "Very well, uncle, I'll apologize to him."

"That's right," said the Prime Minister with great relief; and he fell to his breakfast with an almost cheerful sigh.

The Lady Noggs displayed herself in a most amiable light during the meal. She asked after the country, the continent, the United States of

America, and the Emperor Fritz with a flattering interest. Something in her uncle's tone when he spoke of that last personage awakened her suspicion; and she said quickly, "Has Fritz been behaving badly again?"

In the household of the Prime Minister it was the custom to speak of the Emperor of Transylvania as Fritz, in a pained way, half kindly indulgence, half reproach.

"He has been making himself rather disagreeable," said the Prime Minister reluctantly.

"I never heard of such an Emperor," said the Lady Noggs, shaking her head wisely, "nor did Miss Caldecott. She says that among the Roman Emperors there was no one exactly like him. I asked her. And Billy says that Emperors are a bad lot. I believe he's more trouble to you than me."

"Than I," said the Prime Minister.

"Than I," said the Lady Noggs. "And he never makes up for it by being nice to you afterwards, does he?"

"So far," said the Prime Minister, "I have not found in him any disposition to be nice to me afterwards."

"I wonder," said the Lady Noggs knitting her brow, "if I could do any good, supposing I were to write to him and ask him to behave better."

"No: no good at all," said the Prime Minister quickly, with a very lively dread of some of the papers getting hold of the incident. "I'm afraid he doesn't know how to behave."

"If it's like that, I'm afraid it would be no good," said the Lady Noggs sadly. "But why don't you make him sit up?"

"Make him sit up?" said the Prime Minister, sitting up himself.

"Yes; make him sit up just once — really sit up. He'd behave better after that," said the Lady Noggs earnestly. "I always make them sit up when any one behaves badly to me."

The Prime Minister's face relaxed, and he laughed shortly. "Really, Noggs, there's something in what you say," he said. "Out of the mouths of babes —" And he fell into one of his thoughtful moods.

The Lady Noggs respected his brooding. She devoted herself to her breakfast in silence, only breaking it to say, "Uncle, you are eating a cold chop; those in the dish are hotter," or "Uncle, you're drinking cold coffee; you'd better pour it away and take fresh."

The Prime Minister followed her suggestions

dreamily. When they had done, and were going out of the room, he awoke and said: "You won't forget to apologize to Mr. Borrodaile ?"

"Oh, no; I won't forget. I'm going to do it at once," said the Lady Noggs with a grim smile.

Indeed, she seemed in haste to get it done, for instead of going upstairs and changing her velvet picture gown for the holland frock better adapted to her usual enterprises, which involved no little wear and tear of clothing, she went straight out into the garden.

Mr. Borrodaile was taking his holiday. Smoking his after-breakfast pipe, he was walking up and down a secluded lawn, dreaming. Immersed in his dream, he did not see a violet-clad figure steal up to the entrance of the lawn, and at the sight of him slip into the bushes, and wait in hiding. Presently, as the Lady Noggs, who knew his habits well, expected, he sat down on a seat at the end of the lawn, and continued his reverie drowsily. She worked her way noiselessly round the lawn through the bushes, came out behind him and up to the seat.

The drowsy Mr. Borrodaile felt a soft little hand steal into his hair, and a gentle voice said in his ear, "I apologize about that booby-trap, because uncle told me to, Billy — you sneak!"

And the soft little hand gripped his hair, and gave it a violent tug, which drew from him a yell of anguish.

"I'll teach you to be a sneak," said the Lady Noggs; and she tugged again.

"Drop it, Noggs! Drop it!" roared Mr. Borrodaile.

"Not me," said the Lady Noggs, with little care for her grammar; and she tugged again.

"I'll wring your neck, you little fiend!" roared Mr. Borrodaile; and he had the presence of mind to seize her hand and hold it, so that she could not tug so hard; but more he could not do, for fear of hurting her, and was held a close prisoner.

"Now, you apologize to me for sneaking," said the Lady Noggs, making unavailing efforts to tug.

But at that moment the Prime Minister, attracted by the yells of his secretary, ran into the glade, with a scared face. At first he could not make out what was happening. His secretary lay back in his seat, his face scarlet, groaning, and kicking spasmodically. Behind him stood the Lady Noggs, her eyes shining with righteous triumph.

Both of them were far too deeply absorbed

in the business of the moment to perceive his entry upon the scene until he cried: "Whatever is this? What's the matter, Mr. Borrodaile?"

Lady Noggs looked up, let go Mr. Borrodaile's hair, and said: "I — I was apologizing."

Mr. Borrodaile sprang to his feet, and wiped the tears from his eyes. "Oh, what an ornament to the peerage!" he said bitterly.

"You leave the peerage alone!" cried the Lady Noggs hotly. "I did apologize — I did really, uncle," she went on, turning to the Prime Minister. "Then I pulled his hair for sneaking."

"I should like to know what the beginning of it was," said Mr. Borrodaile irritably. "What did you set the booby-trap for, you — you peeress?"

"She heard you call me a philosopher," said the Prime Minister.

"It's only the truth that wounds," muttered Mr. Borrodaile, feeling softly the booby-trap bump on the top of his head.

The Lady Noggs, thinking that he was feeling the roots of his hair, smiled grimly and said:

"You won't sneak again in a hurry."

"I must insist on your not using this slang, Felicia," said the Prime Minister severely. "I will not have it. Besides, Mr. Borrodaile did not sneak — did not tell me of your unkind trick. I heard the noise myself, and inquired into the matter."

"You didn't sneak? Oh, poor Billy!" said the Lady Noggs. Her face fell; she plumped down on the seat, burst into tears, and wailed, "Oh, I'm a beast! I'm a little beast!"

"You are, Noggs; you are — a perfect little beast," said Mr. Borrodaile, with hearty acquiescence.

But the Prime Minister gazed at the weeping Noggs with every appearance of concern, and said: "Dear, dear, this is very distressing!"

Mr. Borrodaile looked at him with humorous appreciation and said: "She'll be all right soon, sir. Perhaps you'd better go away, and leave her to me. "She'll only be worse with you here."

"Do you think she will?" said the Prime Minister hesitating.

"I'm sure of it. You leave her to me; I understand her."

"Perhaps I'd better. I don't understand children, I'm afraid," said the Prime Minister, and he went hastily, sighing.

Mr. Borrodaile looked at the weeping peeress, and said, with some discomfort: "Now, that's enough, Noggs. I'm appeased, quite appeased. Drop it."

"Poor Billy," sobbed the Lady Noggs. "How I must have hurt you!"

"That's all right. I dare say it was good for my hair. Perhaps it will make it grow."

"No, no; you'll go bald. I know you will."

Mr. Borrodaile put his hand hastily to his head to feel if his hair were already thinning.

The Lady Noggs sobbed on; he fidgetted, and at last said in a tone of disgust: "Don't be so inexpressibly feminine, Noggs. I was hurt, not you."

"I'm not feminine!" cried the Lady Noggs.

"Oh, yes, you are."

"I'm not! I'm not! I'm not!" cried the Lady Noggs.

There was a rustle of skirts, and a very pretty young lady came on to the lawn. Mr. Borrodaile's eyes lighted up at the sight of her, and possibly hers would have lighted up at the sight of Mr. Borrodaile; but they were not allowed.

"Oh, here you are, Noggs," she said in a resigned voice. "I've had the usual hunt for you." Then she saw the child's tear-stained face; turned on Mr. Borrodaile, and said, "What

have you been doing to this child, Mr Borrodaile ?"

"I like that!" cried Mr. Borrodaile. "What
do I ever do to this child ? What has this child
been doing to me, you mean."

"Doing to you ? A child like that!" said Miss
Caldecott.

"Oh, well, she's just explained that she's
made me bald for life," said Mr. Borrodaile
with the air of a cheerful martyr.

"Bald! Good gracious! What has she done ?"

"I pulled his hair out — at least, some of it,"
said the Lady Noggs, looking ruefully at her
guilty fingers, to which stuck a black hair or
two.

"How could you be so cruel, Noggs ?" said
Miss Caldecott.

"I thought he'd sneaked; but he hadn't,"
said the Lady Noggs drying her eyes.

"Poor Mr. Borrodaile," said Miss Caldecott.

"Poor William," said Mr. Borrodaile. "All
my friends call me William."

"Nonsense," said Miss Caldecott, blushing.

"It's quite true," said Mr. Borrodaile. "And
it's a very pretty name. Try it."

"Nonsense," said Miss Caldecott again.

"Well, if you won't," said Mr. Borrodaile,

" Oh, well, she's just explained that she's made me
bald for life "

with a sigh. "But I have been falsely accused, misjudged, and maltreated. My feelings are lacerated. It must be made up to me. I have a holiday to-day. I must be taken on the river — in the Canadian canoe. It holds two."

"Really — some men —" said Miss Caldecott, and paused.

"Oh, you two spoons!" the Lady Noggs broke in with immense contempt.

Miss Caldecott blushed again, turned to her, and said: "My child — there is a little matter of French irregular verbs. You come with me, and apply your extraordinary powers of observation to them."

The Lady Noggs made a wry face and rose. She came up to Mr. Borrodaile, held out her hand, and said, "Shake hands, Billy. We won't have any ill feeling."

Mr. Borrodaile shook hands gravely. "We won't," he said. "But, oh, Noggs, never, never apologise to me again! I don't really care a bit for apologies." And he watched them go.

At the end of the lawn the Lady Noggs bethought herself, paused, turned her head, and shouted back, "Feminine yourself!"

The Lady Noggs had the last word.

CHAPTER TWO

THE SPOILED ADVERTISEMENT

M R. BORRODAILE had too wide a knowledge of the diplomatic method not to make the most of the pity his ill-treatment at the hands of the Lady Noggs had inspired into Miss Caldecott. He descended on her soon after lunch, when she had handed over her distinguished pupil to the entirely nominal care of her nurse Mrs. Greenwood, whose impossible function it was to look after her out of school hours, and had settled herself with a novel in a most comfortable chair under the chestnut trees on the lawn.

She was, to all-seeming, too deeply absorbed in her book to hear his approach, but she did not start when he said in the pathetic tone of one suffering from memories of grievous wrongs, "The Canadian canoe is ready. I've put the cushions in it."

Miss Caldecott lowered her book, and surveyed him with gently inquiring eyes: "Are you going on the river?" she said.

"Yes; I'm going on the river — with you," said Mr. Borrodaile firmly.

"With me?" said Miss Caldecott with every show of surprise.

"Yes," said Mr. Borrodaile. "I need not recapitulate my injuries; they must be fresh in your mind. The time has come for the memory of them to be swept away by pleasanter memories."

Miss Caldecott surveyed him with a good deal of carefully hidden pleasure: his slim but well-knit, flannelled figure, his distinguished face, and honest but somewhat masterful eyes made him a very pleasant sight; but she said, "What have I to do with it? I didn't injure you."

"No; but you have a compassionate heart; and when you see any one cruelly treated, you never rest till you have made it up to them."

"Don't I?"

"Never," said Mr. Borrodaile with supreme conviction. "Besides, you are the only living creature who can sweep away the unhappy memories with pleasant ones."

"A kind of housemaid of the soul," said Miss Caldecott with a whimsical smile.

"Oh, ever so much more than that!" said Mr. Borrodaile with fervour. "The light — the guiding-star — the —"

"The river does sound attractive," said Miss Caldecott hastily. "And if it is in the sacred cause of philanthropy as well." And she rose, and took up her sunshade.

One does not carry a sunshade to read a book on a shady lawn; and Mr. Borrodaile observed the fact with great satisfaction. It seemed to him, however, indiscreet to speak of it. He fell into step beside her, declaring that his poor tortured soul was about to know surcease of sorrow.

At the boat-house, he was helping her into the bow of the canoe so that she faced the stern, when she said somewhat cruelly, "You'd better paddle from the bow, it's easier."

"Impossible," said Mr. Borrodaile. "With my head over my shoulder, for your eyes draw mine like magnets, I should run the canoe against every snag in the river. It wouldn't be safe."

"If you're going to talk nonsense all the time, my philanthropy will be worn out before we've gone a hundred yards, and we shall come straight back."

"I wasn't. But I won't," said Mr. Borro-daile.

He paddled gently out into the middle of the slow stream; and after a short discussion of that inexhaustible theme, the Lady Noggs, they fell to talking of the coming house-party.

"It's a nuisance that that Karskovitch wo-man is coming," said Mr. Borrodaile.

"Why, I thought the party was for her," said Miss Caldecott.

"It is, worse luck," said Mr. Borrodaile gloomily.

"What's the matter with her?"

"I should think that about everything that could be is the matter with her," said Mr. Bor-rodaile more gloomily.

"Tell me about her."

"Well, it's really the Russian government. You know that the paternal government of all the Russias doesn't confine the exercise of its paternal instinct to its own country."

"I thought it did. I thought it never cared anything about any other country."

"In a way it doesn't; but whenever it sees a lonely but influential statesman in another country, it has a way of dropping a pretty lady in his path. Of course it may do it out of mere kindness of heart, to cheer him on his lonely way, don't you know? On the other hand it may do it to get hold of information that doesn't generally go a-begging. It's awfully thirsty for information always is the Russian government."

"I see," said Miss Caldecott thoughtfully.

"It's played this little game — I mean performed this distinguished kindness to English statesmen before, twice. Once it brought it off; once it didn't."

"I know."

"And I think it has noticed the chief's loneliness, and has dropped a pretty lady in his distinctly primrose path. I'm afraid, too, that he's caught."

"What's she like?" said Miss Caldecott quickly.

"She's very pretty and fascinating and clever — too clever. She's the kind of woman who appeals at once to the sympathies of every intellectual sentimentalist; and, between ourselves and this most intelligent canoe, the chief's a good deal of a sentimentalist. She's so clever that I think myself that, like most of these government Russian countesses, she contrived to get born in Montmartre. She's always working her loneliness for all that it's worth, too; and it's a quite genuine appeal, for I can't conceive her producing under any stress of circumstances the Russian count who bears her name."

"Then she's entirely an adventuress."

"Entirely. She came into society by the South African entrance, under the golden wing of Sir Isaac Geltheimer, the mining financier, formerly of Hamburg, now of Park Lane. She met the chief at his house — he always dines there once a year: Sir Isaac is a large contributor to the party funds. She set about fascinating him at once; and she's had every chance of continuing the process. As soon as it was discovered that the chief would go to houses where the Karskovitch was, the Karskovitch was there."

"So he's seen a great deal of her?"

"A great deal too much of her," said Mr. Borrodaile with emphasis.

"Well, it's a good thing that he can't marry her," said Miss Caldecott brightening.

"Not marry her? What's to prevent him?" said Mr. Borrodaile in some surprise.

"Why, her husband."

"Oh, that — I'm expecting every day to hear of the death of Count Karskovitch. I've been sure for nearly a month that he's at his last gasp. These unproduceable husbands die at the most convenient moments."

"You're very cynical," said Miss Caldecott with some severity.

"Well, the world of the Karskovitches is an unsavoury place."

"It's a great pity that Lord Errington should have fallen into her clutches," said Miss Caldecott with a sigh.

"It is. But he'll have to be got out of them — somehow," said Mr. Borrodaile; but his tone was not hopeful.

He paddled on for some time in silence, paying much more attention to the face of his companion than to the course of the canoe. Then with a light in his eyes she knew very well, he began, "Talking about marrying —"

"We won't," said Miss Caldecott quickly.

"It's wonderful how some people shun the most interesting topics," said Mr. Borrodaile with an aggrieved air.

"I am not interested," said Miss Caldecott. But somehow or other before the canoe reached the boat-house again, they, or rather Mr. Borrodaile, had said a good deal on the subject and on subjects akin to it, Miss Caldecott's efforts being chiefly devoted to keeping the conver-

sation on the lines of the general and imper-
sonal.

The Lady Noggs welcomed the prospect of
the house-party with joy. To her, change was
always change; and a house full of people afforded many opportunities. She went for her
usual afternoon ride on the day of the arrival of
her uncle's guests; and they were gathered together at tea when she entered the great hall of
Stonorill Castle with a quiet and stately decorum — induced by the fact that she was accompanied by Miss Caldecott — looking more like
a child after Sir Joshua Reynolds than ever.
Under Miss Caldecott's restraining eye she even
greeted her friends by their proper titles, and
not by the more familiar nicknames of her own
bestowing.

When she came near the Prime Minister, who
was talking to the Countess Karskovitch, he
called her to him, and said, "Countess, this is
my little niece."

In her extravagant foreign fashion, the countess held out both hands, and cried with every appearance of extreme joy, "So this is the wonderful Noggs! Oh, you delightful child! I am so
pleased at last to meet you! I have heard tales
— oh, of the most incredible — about you! We

shall be great friends! oh, great friends! We shall get into mischief together!"

The Lady Noggs looked at the face of the countess with limpid and solemn eyes; she looked at her right hand carefully, and at her left hand with no less care; then she said: "My name is Lady Felicia Grandison. How do you do?" and dropped a deep old-fashioned curtsey.

Two men turned their backs on the group with a simultaneous swift movement; all expression faded from the faces of three women: they stared at nothing with blank eyes.

The countess shut her mouth with a snap; her eyes flashed; and she laughed a laugh which rang quite false. "Truly," she said with a shrug, "you English begin your coldness young."

The Prime Minister frowned upon the Lady Noggs; and then his accurate mind gave him trouble. He could not see which was the right thing, the gushing friendliness of the countess, which showed so plainly a warm and impulsive heart, or the cold dignity of the Lady Noggs. After all the Lady Noggs was the representative of one of the oldest families in England, and she had a right to be coldly dignified if she liked.

"Felicia is not cold as a rule," he said, hardly

" My name is Lady Felicia Grandison. How do you do ? "
and dropped with an old-fashioned curtsey

happily; and then he added quickly, "She is a child of moods."

The Lady Noggs looked at him with a puzzled air, and moved to the tea-table.

"Ah," said the countess plaintively, "We who are alone in the world are so sensitive to coldness." And she sighed.

The Prime Minister made all haste to comfort her.

The Lady Noggs's first instinctive dislike of the countess did not abate, but rather increased, for her eyes were not too young to perceive her uncle's manifest infatuation for the charming creature; and since she regarded him as her peculiar property, her dislike was quickened by jealousy.

Above all she resented the fact that for the first time he abandoned his custom of breakfasting alone with her, and breakfasted with the rest of his guests. Formerly, no matter what guests were in the house, he had clung to the custom which he considered gave the child more of genuine home life. This charming guest changed that; and the Lady Noggs grew jealous indeed. She received all the overtures of the countess with repellent coldness, much to the relief of that charming creature, who would have been very ill at ease trying to play with a child.

Presently, however, the Lady Noggs began to display an open hostility. Miss Caldecott would not allow her to make disparaging remarks about a guest of her uncle; but Mr. Borrodaile was given no choice in the matter, he had to listen to them: the Lady Noggs considered it one of his most important duties. And he heard them with outward equanimity and inward approval; for though, since his chief's social vagaries would be some months filtering through the penny society papers to the ears of the bulk of his strenuous supporters, he was already looking for symptoms of the harm his infatuation for so manifest an adventuress as the countess would do him among the chief men of his party. Yet he awaited the development of events with no little disquiet, since he knew that, with the Lady Noggs, to dislike was to act; and he was sure that her small but active brain was plotting mischief.

This was true; but she could not find her plan. Her wits did not lack stimulant, indeed; the more her uncle basked in the smiles of the countess, the more jealous she grew, and the faster her brain worked. She dismissed the idea of a booby-trap, of an apple-pie bed, and of a string across the stairs: events of this kind were not in the ordinary course of nature, and would at once be ascribed to her human agency. Yet it must be admitted that the scheme which she finally evolved was not much better. The domestic mouse is not of a disposition so adventurous as to scale a dinner-table and conceal itself in a napkin.

Be that as it may, the Prime Minister's guests had seated themselves at table and were unfolding their napkins, when the countess dropped hers, sprang to her feet with a startling scream, stood holding on to the back of her chair gasping and fluttering, while a mouse detached itself from the dropped napkin and with great activity scurried into the bank of ferns which decorated the table. Since the countess had sprung to her feet and screamed, all the other women sat quite still and set their teeth, though they were quivering with an extravagant nervousness. They did not like the countess and they did not like mice, but they liked the countess least. The Duchess of Huddersfield even contrived to say quietly, by a magnificent effort only possible to a woman with generations of well-bred restraint behind her, "Oh, a little mouse."

The men sprang to their feet, with the sportman's ardour gleaming in their eyes; the Marquis of Hartlepool and the Prime Minister supported the trembling countess; the others poked about with their forks among the maiden-hair. Mr. Borrodaile saved the situation and the dinner table; he made a pounce; extracted the mouse by the tail; bore it to the window; and dropped it into the garden.

Each woman moved slightly in her chair with a carefully repressed sigh of relief; the countess sank into hers saying, "My nerves, oh, my nerves! How brave you Englishwomen are! Stoics, true stoics!" And she set about being interesting, with sudden shudders and starts of alarm, for the rest of the evening.

Every one began to suggest theories of how the mouse came to be in the napkin: at least not every one; those who knew the Lady Noggs put forward no theories, and the Prime Minister was frowning.

The next morning the Lady Noggs was summoned to his study before breakfast, and found him frowning still.

"Good-morning, Felicia," he said sternly. "Did you put that mouse in the Countess Karskovitch's napkin last night?"

The Lady Noggs glared at him defiantly, and said curtly, "Yes."

"Dear, dear, what a naughty child you are!" cried the Prime Minister.

"I don't like her," said the Lady Noggs firmly.

"As if that was any reason for playing detestable tricks of this kind on any one! Especially on a guest staying in your house!" cried the Prime Minister.

"It isn't my house! I wouldn't have her in my house!" the Lady Noggs protested vehemently.

The Prime Minister was taken aback: "But, but why do you dislike her so?" he said.

"She's a cat. That's why I gave her the mouse," said the Lady Noggs.

"Really, I can't have this unreasonable behaviour! I will not have you call your elders names, and play these tricks on them! You will go to the Countess Karskovitch and tell her that you are very sorry you did it."

"I'm not sorry. I won't tell her I'm sorry."

The Prime Minister was at a loss: "I insist upon it," he said feebly.

But the Lady Noggs shook her head, and repeated stubbornly, "I'm not sorry. I won't say I'm sorry."

"Well, then," said the Prime Minister, "I shall have to punish you. You will have all your meals in the nursery till the party breaks up."

The Lady Noggs stalked out of the room with a sullen dignity. But once on the other side of the door, she ran upstairs to the nursery, took a new story-book Mr. Borrodaile had given her, a basket, and the doll Grizell, another gift from Mr. Borrodaile, and also of his christening. He had observed that patience was the virtue chiefly needed by the dolls of the Lady Noggs.

She came quietly down the stairs swinging Grizell by the leg, humming a simple nursery lay, with her eyes wider open than usual to show the extreme innocence of her thoughts, the most careless and unconcerned child in the world. She took advantage of the emptiness of the hall to bolt across it, and reached safely the region of the kitchens. In different parts of that region she was seen by several of the servants for about ten minutes, but they were too busy to give any attention to her, and they were not in the habit of questioning her as to her doings, because it was a dangerous thing for the unauthorized to do. She was able therefore to raid the larders successfully, and presently slipped

out into the garden with her basket stocked
with chicken, cake, and pastry.

She went quickly through the gardens, by
side-paths through the shrubberies, until she
came to a broader path which ran alongside a
dense thicket. Half way down it she turned into
the thicket, squeezing her way between two
close-set trees, pushed her way through the
brushwood which closed behind her, and came
into a little clearing on the edge of a long pool.
A fringe of bushes and three or four trees hid
the clearing from any one on the further bank.
This nook was her own discovery; and she had
used it before as a convenient hiding-place in
which to brood at leisure on her wrongs.

She threw the doll Grizell face downwards on
the grass, and set down her basket with a sigh
of relief; then she made herself comfortable
under a tree, and ate her breakfast. When that
was done, she put the uneaten food into the
basket, and set it in the shade; sat for a while
reflecting with vengeful satisfaction on the sorrow her uncle would feel on learning that he
had driven her away; then got to business.

She set the doll Grizell up against a tree,
looking across the pool and said: "Now, idiot,
I'm an enchanted princess in her bower, wait-

ing for the prince to come, and you're my lady-in-waiting. And there are lots and lots of wicked enchanters and witches hunting for me. But if we keep quiet, they'll never see us, never. You're to keep watch for them and at any rate I shan't see your silly face."

With that she lay down on the moss and began to read her story-book. Now and again she looked up at Grizell to see if she were discharging faithfully her duty, and once she rose and thoughtfully banged that patient creature's head against the tree by way of quickening her sense of responsibility.

After breakfast the Prime Minister sent for Miss Caldecott and informed her of the punishment to which he had condemned her pupil.

"Then she didn't breakfast with you?" said Miss Caldecott with some dismay.

"No; didn't she breakfast with you?" said the Prime Minister.

"I haven't seen her since you sent for her, and I shouldn't wonder if I didn't see her for the rest of the day. She has a hiding-place to which she retires when her dignity is ruffled. She has done it twice this summer, and I cannot find out where it is."

"Dear, dear!" said the Prime Minister. "Why

wasn't I told of this?" And he took hold of his beard with both hands, and held it firmly, for comfort.

"If I told you of all Nog — Lady Felicia's pranks, I'm afraid you would have little time to think of anything else," said Miss Caldecott smiling. "But, of course, I punish her for these retreats."

"Yes, yes," said the Prime Minister; "you are quite right. What I hear of her doings gives me trouble enough. A very difficult child."

"Oh, no: not at all," said Miss Caldecott cheerfully. "She is very honest and good-hearted, and obedient, as children go, if I tell her to do or not to do anything. The difficulty is to be quick enough with the bidding or forbidding, to anticipate the workings of her ingenious mind. But I had better go at once and try to find her."

The Prime Minister let go his beard, and sighed. "It's very tiresome," he said, "very tiresome."

The Lady Noggs was not found. She passed a restful day in her capacity of princess in an enchanted bower. She read her story-book, she ate, she slept, and now and again she discussed frankly, apparently with the circumambient air, the doll Grizell's lamentable lack of intelligence. Late in the morning and again in the afternoon she enjoyed the diversion of observing different people, servants and guests, hunting for her. She did not hear them, for as soon as their far-off, indistinguishable crying reached her ears, she thrust her fingers into them that she might be able to say truthfully that she had heard no one call her name. She observed that Miss Caldecott and Mr. Borrodaile hunted together, and regarded Mr. Borrodaile's air of absorbed devotion with infinite scorn.

Now it chanced that a grievance had been rankling in the mind of the Countess Karskovitch. She had been feeling, with a genuine bitterness, that her intimacy with the Prime Minister was by no means duly advertised. Then she had hit upon the happy but hardly original idea of having her jewels stolen. To the surprise of the Lady Noggs, at about six o'clock, just when her enchanted but solitary occupation was beginning to pall, she saw her enemy on the further bank of the pool, alone. She watched at first carelessly, and then with all her eyes. The countess carried a packet, and, to the surprise of the Lady Noggs, after a hasty glance back along the path by which she had come, she knelt down by a willow, lowered the packet into the water by a string, and tied it to one of the roots of the tree. Then she rose, looked sharply round, and went back towards the house.

The curiosity of the Lady Noggs was far too keen for her not to risk discovery, she stole to the end of the thicket, bolted from it to the willow, unfastened the string, hauled up the packet and bolted back with it to her lair. She went right back to her bower before she examined her salvage, and then found it to be a small reticule. She made no bones about opening it, and found to her surprise that it contained a diamond tiara, necklace, star, bracelets, and rings. At least, her inexpert, childish eyes took the stones for diamonds; really, in equipping the countess for its little deed of kindness, the paternal instinct of the Russian government had only run to paste.

The Lady Noggs was no longer bored; she played for a long time with her treasure-trove, decking herself with the ornaments and wishing that she had a mirror to see the effect. So long did she play that the countess, after forcing open her empty jewel-case with a screw-driver, and locking her bedroom door, was coming down to dinner with the other guests, when she reached the castle. She went up to her room by a back staircase, hoping to reach it unobserved, but Miss Caldecott was expecting her, caught her, scolded her severely, and sent her to bed at once without any supper. She took the scolding and the punishment with unusual meekness, and escaped to her own room with the reticule.

Her lack of supper, and the fact that she had slept during the day, kept her awake. It was nearly ten o'clock when she heard a great stir in the house, hurrying footsteps and people talking in high, excited tones. Then she heard Mr. Borrodaile knock at the door of Miss Caldecott's sitting-room, which adjoined her bedroom, enter and say, "Here's a pretty to-do! The countess has been robbed of her jewels!"

"How ?" cried Miss Caldecott.

" It seems as if the burglars had set up a ladder, climbed into her bedroom window, and forced open her jewel-case, while we were at dinner."

"What are you going to do ?"

"Oh, we're sending word to the police at Warlesden — not that they will be of much use — to send a man over, and wire for a detective from Scotland Yard."

The Lady Noggs waited to hear no more; she saw that the intervention of a capable person was called for; jumped out of bed, put on her dressing-gown and slippers, took the reticule from under the mattress, and hurried out of the room. She was already at the head of the staircase when Miss Caldecott and Mr. Borrodaile came out of the sitting-room to see what was going on, saw her, and hurried after her.

The Lady Noggs ran down to the staircase into the great hall, and, hearing a buzz of talk from the library, made for it. She found her uncle and most of his guests in it; and as she entered, the countess, who sat at the end of the table, was saying plaintively: "They were heirlooms, the family jewels of the Karskovitches. My husband gave them to me in the earlier days of our married life — the happy days."

There was a murmur of sympathy from the men: the Lady Noggs slipped through a commiserating group, said scornfully, "Here are your old jewels!" and threw the sodden reticule on to the table.

There was an outcry from those who stood round; and the face of the countess, set fixed as it was, in the middle of a plaintive smile. In all the world, the reticule was the last object she desired to see at that moment; and she stared at the abhorred object as she might have stared at a striking cobra. But the Duke of Huddersfield, who stood by the table, picked it up, opened it, and poured the glittering trinkets on the table. "Are they all right?" he said, turning them over.

His action gave the countess time; she got her breath, and looked sorrowfully at the Lady Noggs: she said, "Oh, what a cruel child, to give me such a fright!"

"What fright?" said the Lady Noggs, puzzled.

"It's really monstrous that you should play such a trick, Felicia!" cried the Prime Minister angrily.

"Stealing jewels, even for a joke, is a bit thick," said a young admirer of the countess.

"Stealing!" cried the Lady Noggs hotly. "I didn't steal them! They weren't stolen at all! She hid them herself in the White Pool, at the bottom of the garden. I was hiding on the other side of it. I'd been there all day. I saw her let down the reticule by a string tied to a willow-root, and I fished it out."

"Oh, what a wicked child! to play a trick, and then tell a lie about it!" cried the countess, at bay.

" Oh, what a wicked child ! to play a trick, and then tell
a lie about it ! "

"Dear, dear, this is very distressing!" said the Prime Minister.

Suddenly Miss Caldecott stood beside the Lady Noggs, her pretty face flushed and indignant. "It's absurd!" she cried in a very clear ringing voice, "Lady Felicia never tells lies!"

"It's nonsense!" said Mr. Borrodaile over Miss Caldecott's shoulder, "Noggs never lies!"

"Besides," said Miss Caldecott, "the countess says the jewels were lost during dinner. Nogg — Lady Felicia was in her bedroom all dinner time. I can answer for it."

"Ah, the amiable governess and secretary! Is it a plot?" said the countess with a faint sneer.

It was a hopelessly false step. Mr. Borrodaile was a relation or connection of half the people in the room. There was a murmur; and the group about the countess drew a little away.

"It's quite true," said the Lady Noggs, still a little bewildered.

"Mon dieu! What a wicked child! Or has she been taught the story?" cried the countess. "What motive, what possible motive could I have for doing such a thing?"

"Advertisement," said Mr. Borrodaile promptly, but curtly.

The magic word cleared the air; there was a smothered laugh or two, and a good deal of coughing.

One look at the Prime Minister's stern face showed the countess that the game was lost, and she rose to the situation. With the air of a tragedy queen she sprang to her feet, and cried, "So this is your English hospitality! You plot the ruin of a defenceless woman! And use a little child as the instrument of your baseness! Let me go! I will have no more to do with you. Curs!"

She swept down the room, and was making an excellent exit, when she spoiled everything by turning on the Lady Noggs as she passed and crying, "Oh, you wicked and abominable child!"

The Lady Noggs had at last grasped in all its fulness the nefarious attempt of the countess, and she was indeed angry. "I'm not!" she cried fiercely. "You're a wicked woman! And one of these days you'll go to prison, and they'll wash your face, and you won't have any complexion!"

The Lady Noggs had the last word.

CHAPTER THREE

SIX RABBITS A WEEK

IT might have been an acute consciousness of virtue, in that she had been the instrument of the exposure of the adventurous Countess Karskovitch. It might have been that a whole day of peace in her bower had induced a passing restfulness of disposition. It might have been lack of opportunity. But for a long while, quite three weeks, the Lady Noggs suffered her elders to enjoy a grateful and unlooked-for peace. During all that time she only ruined two frocks, and that without a general upheaval of Stonorill life. The fact that her next exploit destroyed a pair of stockings as well as a frock, and narrowly missed compelling the dwellers in the castle to spend a sleepless night hunting for her, was the fault of Mr. Borrodaile.

When one morning she joined him after breakfast, as he was smoking a cigarette before dealing with the Prime Minister's correspondence, she had no thought of stirring out of the gardens that day. But since he and Miss Caldecott had been talking of the uneventful lives the neighbourhood had lived of late, the subject was in his mind, and he said idly, but with unpardonable carelessness, "Are you feeling quite all right, Noggs?"

The Lady Noggs considered the matter carefully for half a minute, and said, "Yes; thank you."

"You're sure?" said Mr. Borrodaile.

"Quite. Why?" said the Lady Noggs.

"Oh, you've been so quiet lately. I was wondering if you felt out of sorts."

The Lady Noggs seemed to plunge into deep thought; then she said, "Yes; I have been very quiet. But you ought to be very glad, Billy. It gives you and Violet such a lot of time to spoon."

Mr. Borrodaile flushed a little, and said with some warmth, "Don't talk nonsense!" Even a philosopher would not hear with indifference the natural and irrepressible manifestation of his impassioned devotion called spooning; and Mr. Borrodaile had not reached philosophic years.

"It isn't nonsense," said the Lady Noggs firmly. "You think I don't see but I do."

"I wonder where you got that vulgar word
from — spooning. It does sound well in the
mouth of an ornament of the peerage," said
Mr. Borrodaile scornfully.

"I got it from you, Billy. It was you who said
that Mr. Brampton was spooning in the con-
servatory with Miss Marjoribanks. And you
said it in one of your nasty sneering ways. But
that was before you began spooning yourself."

Mr. Borrodaile was aware that he had been
severely defeated; but his political training
stood him in good stead, and he said coldly, "I
wonder why it is you always pick up some word
like that from my conversation, when you have
so many admirable words and phrases to choose
from. Can there be some painful tendency towards the diction of the lower classes in your
disposition? If so, check it, Noggs. Check it, I
implore you."

The Lady Noggs made no direct reply to the
suggestion. She walked quietly towards the
house, and as she went she sang softly, but on a
singularly taunting note, "Spoon! Spoon! Spoon!
— Spoon! Spoon! Spoon!"

The suggestion that she had a tendency to
acquire a vulgar diction gave the Lady Noggs

no concern; but now that her attention had been so pointedly drawn to the quietness of the life she had been leading, her thoughts, naturally, turned to adventure. With that end in view no sooner had she finished lunch than she was off. There was generally in her day a few minutes' interregnum between her passing from the charge of Miss Caldecott to the charge of Mrs. Greenwood. Of this interval she now took advantage to put a comfortable distance between herself and both of them, and was in the heart of the Stonorill woods some time before her worthy nurse had quite grasped the fact that she had an afternoon's search before her.

The Lady Noggs had gone but a little way when her high, adventurous spirit was somewhat ruffled by a meeting with Morton, her uncle's head-keeper. His was a grudging soul; and he had a theory, not wholly baseless, that the Lady Noggs was more injurious to his gamekeeping, by disturbing the nesting birds on her explorations of the woods, than all the foxes, polecats, badgers, stoats, hawks, jays, and magpies who preyed on them or their eggs.

As they met, he said with gruff surliness, "Now, your ladyship, what are you a-doing of here? You know very well as how his lordship

has forbid you trapsing about the woods in nesting time."

"I'm not in the woods. I'm on the drive,"
said the Lady Noggs, who was always so much
more careful of the letter than of the spirit of
any prohibition.

"And long you'll be on it! I shall just come
along of you, and see as how you keep to the
drive till you're through the wood," said Morton, and he turned and trudged along beside
her.

The Lady Noggs was very angry indeed at
the open display of an unfounded lack of confidence; and for a while she said nothing. Then,
having recovered her temper, she said in her
sweetest voice, "Has your nose always been like
that, Morton ?"

It chanced that Morton suffered from the
sensitive delicacy of the unlucky in love about
his personal appearance. No one had ever before urged anything against the prominent feature — or perhaps "feature" is too strong a
word, "projection" would be more accurate —
against the prominent projection in his face, so
that hitherto he had never doubted it; but now
his mind misgave him. He pondered the shape of
his nose with a growing disquiet, and more and

more strongly he wished that the Lady Noggs
had been more explicit. The vagueness of the
suggestion of lack of symmetry made it the more
discomfiting. But the Lady Noggs had no intention of being more explicit, for that would
have shown a lack of politeness; and she had,
in truth, nothing against the nose, which was to
the eye much as other rustic noses. She had, so
to speak, shot an arrow in the air, by way of a
just punishment for unfounded distrust, and
her mind moved to other matters. But when she
had climbed over the gate at the end of the wood,
she turned and with painful thoughtfulness said,
"I'm very sorry for you, Morton."

She went briskly along the footpath over the
fields, and Morton watched her go. Then he
turned back into the wood, and as he went he
felt his nose, cautiously, many times.

The Lady Noggs came to the end of the fields
and on to a waste common. She crossed it, and
just as she was entering the copse on the further
side of it, a magpie flew out of an ancient tree.
Now she knew that a single magpie is the har-
binger of ill luck; but instead of turning back,
she went into the copse, and began to examine
the tree from every side. Her sharp eyes presently discovered the magpie's nest. She had

never seen a magpie's nest or a magpie's egg,
and her lively curiosity was at once awakened.
A minute after her curiosity was awakened she
was climbing the ancient tree.

It was gnarled and well furnished with short
stumps of broken branches: her skirt and one
stocking were torn in the ascent; also she
scratched her face. When she came into the
top of the tree, the nest was still some fifteen
feet above her, and at the height of another six
feet she found herself on swaying, shaky boughs.
She sought in vain for one to bear her weight,
but found none: the magpies had known their
business too well. She looked at the nest in disgusted disappointment for a while. Then she
began to descend.

But it is one thing to climb up an ancient tree,
and quite another to climb down it. At some
forty feet from the ground she found herself
stuck. She could not see how to compass the
next eight feet without tumbling the next thirty
to the ground. Twice she worked round the
trunk without finding a way; then she essayed
the least dangerous, found herself slipping, and
lost a shoe in the frantic struggle which brought
her back to safety. She seated herself in a fork,
recovering her breath, and summing up the

salient points of an unpleasant situation. With her scratched face, tousled hair, torn frock and stockings, and shoeless foot, she bore but little of her usual resemblance to a child after Sir Joshua Reynolds, but was very much more like one of the little girls who dance to the strains of a barrel-organ in the purlieus of Soho. In fact she only differed from such an one in the gloominess of her expression. It was not unnatural, for she faced the far from alluring prospect of spending a cheerless but airy night on her perch.

The copse was far from a road. There was little likelihood of any one coming that way; the search for her would begin before her bedtime, since her many truancies had accustomed the servants to look no sooner for her return. It would not become vigorous for an hour after that; and the searchers would scarcely spread so far out from the castle before the morrow. She was helpless; and after a vindictive glance at the magpie's nest, which had lured her up the tree and then proved inaccessible, she settled down to a gloomy musing.

She mused for a long while, rousing herself at intervals to look out with a searching but hopeless glance across the country. It was always empty. Then to her extreme surprise her eyes, returning from one of these glances, fell on a man standing in the copse itself not thirty yards from her. He must have slipped into it from the gorse on the common, and noiselessly. She was so surprised that she did not at once call out, and had time to gather that he was engaged in the time-honoured business of poaching: at least he dived into a bush, pulled a rabbit out of it, divested deftly its neck of a snare, and dropped it into his pocket.

"Hi!" cried the Lady Noggs.

The man jumped, and stared round him with a scared face; and the Lady Noggs recognized William Cotteril, a young labourer who had belied the promise of his bachelorhood by earning for himself as a married man the reputation of a ne'er-do-well.

"Don't stand there, stupid!" cried the Lady Noggs. "Come and help me out of this tree."

William Cotteril discovered whence the voice came, and drew near gingerly, opening his mouth to get a better view of the tree. He stared up and at last distinguished the face of the Lady Noggs. "Why drat me!" he said, "If it ain't her little ladyship!"

"Don't stand talking there, silly! Come and

help me down!" cried the Lady Noggs, wildly impatient at the prospect of deliverance.

William Cotteril plunged into the tree, and, from the noise he made, seemed to be kicking himself heavenwards with very large boots. At last his round and shining face appeared at the bottom of the impracticable eight feet; and the Lady Noggs cried, "Stop there! Don't climb any higher, or you'll get stuck too! This is the bit I can't get down."

William Cotteril drew himself on to a bough and examined the bit with the eye of an expert: "It is a bit orkud," he said, scratching his head. "Do you think as 'ow if I stood up and 'eld on to the trunk, you could climb down me, your ladyship ?"

"Of course I could," said the Lady Noggs with decision.

Accordingly, William Cotteril stood on his bough and embraced the trunk of the tree. The Lady Noggs lowered herself slowly till her feet rested firmly on his shoulders, scrambled down the rest of him, and stood on the broad bough beside him. "That's all right," she said with a sigh of relief.

The rest of the descent presented no difficulties to her, and she was at the bottom and putting on her fallen shoe by the time William reached the ground.. "Well, you be a nimble kiddie, I mean young lady, begging your ladyship's pardon," he said respectfully.

The Lady Noggs rose, stamped her foot firmly into her shoe, and said, with all the aggressive virtue of a person who has come safely out of wrongdoing, "You were poaching, William Cotteril."

"Now, don't go for to say that, your ladyship, just becos I 'appened to pick up a dead rabbit wot was bein' wasted lyin' there," said William with a very fair imitation of the virtuous man wrongfully accused.

"Yes, in a snare. I saw it," said the Lady Noggs; and she set out towards the castle.

William Cotteril walked beside her, and now and again he scratched his head to quicken the action of his brain. At last he said, "Begging your ladyship's pardon, but if so be as you wouldn't say nothing about that rabbit, I should take it kindly."

"I shan't say anything about the rabbit, because I never tell tales," said the Lady Noggs proudly.

"Thank you, your ladyship," said William with a grunt of relief.

"You've no business to poach, William," said the Lady Noggs, still aggressively virtuous. "It's very wrong. One of these days you'll get caught and go to prison. Why don't you do honest work?"

"Honest work?" cried William Cotteril, suddenly purple with the bursting forth of a grievance. "Why don't I do honest work? I can't get it, your ladyship! Morton 'e's gone an' give me a bad name; and I can't get no work. He's poisoned Mr. McNaghten agin me, and not a farmer about 'ere durstn't give me no work, not reg'lar work, only a job at 'arvesting or 'aymaking. They 'as to stand well with Mr. McNaghten, him bein' his lordship's agent, an' they know 'e wants me out o' the village. But I won't go! My feyther 'e lies in Stonorill churchyard, an 'is feyther, an 'is feyther afore 'im. They all lived in the cottage, an' as long as I pays my rent they can't turn me out of it. An' one way an' another I scrapes it together. An' it's all that there Morton's doing."

"What did he do it for?" said the Lady Noggs.

"Well, 'e was sweet on Liza afore I married 'er. An' now 'e's got a grudge agin us. Why I'd never took so much as a rabbit till 'e told Mr.

McNaghten I was a poacher; but when I found
as I'd got the name, I thought I'd do summut to
earn it."

The Lady Noggs filled with sympathy for
William. She was so often rightfully accused
that to be wrongfully accused, as sometimes
befell her, soured her naturally amiable disposition for a good half hour, and she understood
William's feelings. Moreover he, too, was an
enemy of Morton.

"An' after all," said the worthy William,
"what is it I takes? A rabbit or two to make
Liza a drop of broth till she's stronger."

"Is she ill?" said the Lady Noggs quickly.

"Yes; she's ailing, your ladyship. Nursing
the little un it's pulled 'er down."

For a hundred yards the Lady Noggs said
nothing; then she asked, "Would a rabbit a day
be enough?"

"Lor' bless yer, your ladyship, 'eaps. Why I
only 'ad two rabbits last week and three the
week afore that."

"Well," said the Lady Noggs thoughtfully,
"I'll give you a rabbit a day; that is all but Sundays. It's wrong to catch rabbits on Sundays."

"Thank you, your ladyship," said William
doubtfully.

The Lady Noggs was too quick not to notice the doubt in his tone, and she said, "If I can't manage it, I'll let you know."

"Thank you, your ladyship," said William more cheerfully. "Six rabbits a week would pay the rent as well as make broth for Liza."

At the cross-roads they bade one another good-night; she took the way to the castle, he to the village.

The Lady Noggs went thoughtfully, and now and again she smiled. She could see her way, at any rate, to annoy the grumpy and inimical Morton. When she reached the castle, a brief consideration of her dilapidated appearance assured her that the moment she came under the eye of Miss Caldecott she would be sent supperless to bed. Therefore she slipped in at a side entrance, gained the kitchen, beguiled an omelette and three kinds of indigestible sweets from the cooks, and sat on a kitchen table to eat them. Thus fortified she confronted Miss Caldecott, who sent her to bed at sight.

The next day the Lady Noggs by no means assailed her uncle the Prime Minister at breakfast, when he had the leisure to discuss matters at length. She waited till after lunch, and rushed into the library just as that unfortunate statesman, having dealt with affairs of state till the afternoon post should come in, had settled down to the perusal of one of the obscure but German philosophers he loved. He greeted her entry with a sigh, for the Fates alone could determine how much of his scanty leisure she would waste.

The Lady Noggs flitted about the room looking like a charming and gorgeous butterfly, for to Miss Caldecott's extreme surprise she had for once delayed getting into a holland frock immediately after lunch. While she flitted, she discoursed amiably of trifles till she had heard her uncle sigh twice more. Then she said briskly, "Uncle, I want some rabbits, six rabbits a week."

"Six rabbits a week! Three hundred and twelve rabbits a year! Wherever will you keep them?" cried the Prime Minister.

"Oh, I don't want those silly, tame, lumpy ones," said the Lady Noggs. "I want wild rabbits — rabbits to eat."

"But you are never going to eat a rabbit a day!" cried the Prime Minister; and the perplexity deepened on his face.

"No; I don't want them for myself — I want them for a poor family. You might let me have them: there are hundreds in the park."

The Prime Minister was delighted at this sudden development of the instinct of benevolence in his niece, but painful experience of her many-sided mind had made him a trifle distrustful, and he said, "What poor family?"

"That's a secret," said the Lady Noggs firmly. "But do give them to me. If I change quick, I've time for a ride before tea."

The face of the Prime Minister shone with a sudden extreme brightness: "Certainly, certainly," he said quickly: "You can have them." And he turned joyfully to his book.

"I should like them in writing," said the Lady Noggs.

"Rabbits in writing?" said the Prime Minister in a fresh bewilderment.

"Yes; you might be away, and Morton make a fuss about it, and say they weren't mine. He's so disagreeable."

"Oh, I understand," said the Prime Minister. "You want me to make them over to you by a written document." And, greedy for another dose of German thoughtfulness, he wrote hastily,

"Lady Felicia has my permission to have six rabbits a week.

"ERRINGTON."

He smiled at the document as he gave it to the Lady Noggs; and she smiled, too, but quite differently. Then she blew him a kiss, and went.

Apparently she changed her mind about going for a ride, for she ran up to her room, put on a picture-hat, and went out into the park. There she contrived to come across Morton on his way to the woods. He passed her grumpily without a glance: the matter of his nose, which his mirror had left unsettled, was rankling. But she stopped, and said sweetly, "Morton, you forgot to touch your hat."

Morton mumbled something in his throat, and hit the brim of his hat with a spasmodic jerk that knocked it off.

"You should never forget little things, Morton," said the Lady Noggs, with a happy remembrance of the teaching of Miss Caldecott, and she added even more sweetly, "And, oh, I wish William Cotteril to have six rabbits a week. If you see him catching them, you needn't interfere with him."

Morton could only grunt.

"I thought I'd better tell you," said the Lady Noggs.

"I knows my dooty, and I does it," said Morton stormily, and passed on.

Later in the day the Lady Noggs went down
to the village and called upon the Cotteril family. She showed a lively interest in the baby and
talked to Mrs. Cotteril; then she informed William that she had arranged for him to have the
six rabbits a week. Before she left them she gave
Mrs. Cotteril half-a-crown out of her weekly
five shillings pocket money, which even in that
sparsely inhabited country district she contrived always to spend before the next Tuesday
afternoon. In consequence of this charitable im-
pulse she was that week very short of money;
but this shortness was more than made up to
her by the satisfying glow of hope which warmed
her whenever she saw the unsuspecting Morton.

For two or three weeks the Cotteril family
enjoyed a comparatively affluent prosperity:
William had three or four days work and six
rabbits a week. On every Saturday afternoon
the Lady Noggs presented Mrs. Cotteril with
half-a-crown. But in a small village such a
change to affluence as that experienced by the
Cotterils does not escape the neighbourly eye,
or the smell of stewing the rabbit the neighbourly nose; and some warm-hearted friend of
William informed Morton that it might be
worth his while to keep an eye on him.

Then, on a red-letter day when the Lady Noggs had behaved so well and torn her frock so little that she had been actually allowed to have her supper in the nursery, a maid came to tell her that Mrs. Cotteril wanted to speak to her, and was waiting in the servants' hall. The Lady Noggs made haste to finish her supper, and hurried down-stairs. She found Mrs. Cotteril with her baby in her arms, looking thinner and wanner than ever, and crying softly.

"Good-evening, Mrs. Cotteril," said the Lady Noggs. "What's the matter?"

"Good-evening, your ladyship, please your ladyship, John Lubbock, the constable, and Morton has taken William off to the lockup at Warlesden for snaring a rabbit; and he told me to come to you at once and tell you, and maybe you could help him," said Mrs. Cotteril; but she showed no hopefulness at all.

"Didn't he tell them that I had given him leave to have six rabbits a week?" said the Lady Noggs.

"Yes, he did, your ladyship, and they laughed."

The Lady Noggs flushed a little and her nostrils dilated. "They laughed, did they?" she said shortly. "Didn't they say anything about coming to me to ask if it was true?"

"No, your ladyship," said Mrs. Cotteril in a more hopeless tone than ever. "They only laughed. And William he'll be had up before the Bench to-morrow, and they'll send him to prison, and me and the baby will have to go to the Union, and we'll lose the cottage and have to leave the village. It'll break William's 'eart, I know it will!" She ended in a wail, and again sobbed bitterly.

The Lady Noggs was taken aback; she had expected Morton to come to her and ask if William's statement was true, so that she would have had the pleasure of showing him her uncle's letter and enjoying his discomfiture. It had never occurred to her that Morton would pay so little regard to her authority as not even to think it worth his while to inquire into the matter of the truth of William's story that she had given him the rabbits. For the while she could not see, though she cudgelled her brains her hardest, how to deal with this unexpected situation. However, Mrs. Cotteril's grief and fear had to be soothed. She patted her on the arm therefore, and said firmly, " Don't you cry, I'll see that William doesn't go to prison."

Mrs. Cotteril shook her head: "They won't

pay any 'eed to your ladyship, you're so young," she sobbed.

"Oh, yes, they will," said the Lady Noggs, "the magistrates know me so well; and that makes such a difference."

She went on with her encouragement and assurances, proffering them with confidence so catching that, after a while, she had Mrs. Cotteril almost comforted and hopeful, and eating supper sent from the kitchens with a show of appetite. Only when the poor woman had gone, and she herself was in bed, did the mind of the Lady Noggs grapple fairly with the crisis. She puzzled and puzzled over it, striving to find a way of dealing with it "all herself," and was awake for nearly an hour before she formed her plan.

After breakfast with her uncle next morning, she took advantage of his absorption in his newspaper to slip quickly out of the breakfast room, and said to a footman burnishing armour in the hall, "Will you please tell Sykes to put Phelim in the dog-cart as quickly as he can, Symons: and he needn't bring him round; he's to go in to Warlesden."

Thinking that she brought instructions straight from her uncle, Symons made haste, passed them on as coming from him; and when ten minutes later she climbed into the dog-cart, and bade the groom drive quickly to Warlesden, the groom took it that she had leave to go.

It was half past ten before they drew up in front of the offices of the Urban District Council of the sleepy little town, where the magistrates were sitting.

The Lady Noggs made no unseemly haste; she climbed down from the dog-cart, told the groom to wait for her, and entered the justice-room with the calm, deliberate air of a born ruler of men. William Cotteril stood between two policemen; and she gave him a nod and a smile which brightened a little his gloomy face. Then she saw her enemy Colonel Stiffgate of Stiffgate, who believed as firmly as Morton that her explorations of his woods injured his game, sitting at the table; but, confident in the justice of her cause, the sight did not dismay her. Then she saw one of her greatest friends, Sir Hildebrand Wyse, sitting by Colonel Stiffgate's side, and she was assured of victory. She smiled a greeting to Sir Hildebrand; he rose, and, coming to her, shook hands, and asked her what fortunate errand brought her there.

"Oh," said the Lady Noggs, "I know all

about William Cotteril's poaching, and I came to tell you."

"Well, we are just hearing about it," said Sir Hildebrand; and he set a chair for her at the table.

As she sat down, Colonel Stiffgate growled something about the court being no place for children.

The Lady Noggs, sure of the support of Sir Hildebrand, looked at him with infinite coldness; and Sir Hildebrand said carelessly, "It's all right, Stiffgate, Lady Grandison knows something about this poaching business; besides, as you ought to know, if she's made up her mind to hear our proceedings, she'll probably manage to hear them somehow, even if she had to climb up and look through the ventilator."

Colonel Stiffgate growled something about what would happen to her if she were a child of his, and sharply bade Morton get on with his evidence, which her coming had interrupted.

Morton, whom many poaching cases had made an excellent witness, told the story of his watching William Cotteril snare and carry off a rabbit, in an entirely convincing style.

"Monstrous! monstrous!" cried Colonel

Stiffgate, the bright warm, even red of his complexion deepening with all a game-preserver's fury. "What have you to say for yourself, prisoner? Monstrous! monstrous!"

"Her little ladyship there give me the rabbits," said William Cotteril, with the sullen air of a poor man exceedingly doubtful of getting justice from the great Unpaid.

"Little Lady Grandison! Gave you the rabbits! What do you mean? What cock-and-bull story is this?" cried Colonel Stiffgate.

"She give me the rabbits. Six rabbits a week she said I might have," said William Cotteril stubbornly.

"It's quite right. I gave them to him," said the Lady Noggs in her clear voice.

"But *how* could Lady Grandison give you the rabbits? They are Lord Errington's rabbits? It's nonsense — nonsense!" roared Colonel Stiffgate, ignoring the Lady Noggs.

"She give them to me," said William Cotteril with a touch of despair in his stubbornness.

"Do you know anything of this, Mr. McNaghten?" said Colonel Stiffgate to the agent, who sat in a corner watching the case. "Has little Lady Grandison any authority to dispose of Lord Errington's rabbits?"

"None that I am aware of," said Mr. Mc-
Naghten. "And she would hardly have been invested with such authority without my being
informed of it."

"I thought not! I thought not! A cock-and-
bull story! It only makes your offence worse,
prisoner — an impudent plea!"

"They were my rabbits to do as I liked with!"
broke in the Lady Noggs fiercely. "Uncle gave
them to me!" And she gave a somewhat dirty
and crumpled sheet of paper to Sir Hildebrand
Wyse.

"I think her ladyship is making a mistake,"
said Mr. McNaghten suavely.

"Of course, of course. People don't give little
girls rabbits — wild rabbits," said Colonel Stiffgate. "And you knew it, prisoner. You knew it
as well as I. It aggravates your offence; and I
shall make an example of —"

"Hold on, Stiffgate! hold on!" said Sir Hilde-
brand Wyse in a low sharp voice. "Lady Nogg
— Grandison is quite right: the rabbits are hers.
Look at this."

Colonel Stiffgate took the document, and read
it slowly. The wrath of the game-preserver,
balked of his poaching prey, swelled his heart;
he looked round the room for some one to vent

it on, and his eye fell on the luckless Morton, who was smirking at having at last ruined his rival.

"I wish," said the purple Stiffgate thickly, "that you Stonorill people would show a spark of ordinary intelligence in the management of your affairs. What do you mean, keeper — " his voice rose to a sudden terrifying bellow — "by wasting the time of the Bench by a trumpery charge like this? Here is a letter from Lord Errington himself, giving Lady Grandison the rabbits!"

"I — I didn't know nothing about it," stammered Morton.

"You didn't know, you thick-headed lout of a fool!" bellowed the purple Stiffgate. "You ought to have known, you confounded numskull! It's your business to know, blockhead! Not to come wasting my time with trumpery charges like this! The prisoner is discharged! The next case!"

William Cotteril shuffled out of the court with a somewhat dazed air; Morton slunk out after him. The Lady Noggs lingered to tell Sir Hildebrand Wyse how that this was the upshot of William's marrying Morton's sweetheart.

She came out of the building between two

She came out of the building between two groups

groups. On the right hand was a group of Stonorill villagers who had cheerfully walked seven
miles to see William sent to prison, and were
now congratulating him in the half-hearted
manner of the disappointed. On the left a group
of far more joyful persons was repeating to Morton, in case it should not have impressed itself
thoroughly on his mind, the tribute of the purple
Stiffgate to his intelligence. As the Lady Noggs
came out, she heard him say, "To think that
that dratted brat should have made a fool o' me
afore the Bench like that!"

The words "dratted brat" stuck in the Lady
Noggs's mind, but she received the thanks of
William Cotteril with a pretty graciousness,
and told him to climb up on to the back seat of
the dog-cart, that he might as quickly as possible
bring home himself to his anxious wife the good
news of his deliverance.

Then she climbed into the dog-cart, turned
round, and said in a clear, dispassionate voice
heard by every one, "Morton, I didn't make a
fool of you. Nobody could. You grew so."

The Lady Noggs had the last word.

CHAPTER FOUR

THE LADY NOGGS FLAGS THE
NORTHERN STAR

THE LADY NOGGS did not rest content with the rescue of William Cotteril from the greedy grip of the law. His wife's grief on the occasion of his arrest had brought home, even to her childish understanding, the wretched circumstances of the family. Her pity was soon reinforced by the fact that she began to take great pleasure in playing the part of Lady Bountiful; and she gave all her energies to improving their condition. She thought at first of enlisting the sympathies of her uncle and Mr. Borrodaile on their behalf; but her fondness for doing things "all herself" prevented her. Besides, experience had shown her that, with busy men like her uncle and Mr. Borrodaile, action was slow. In the political sphere it might be quicker, for anything she knew; but she wanted the Cotterils relieved at once; and she was sure that there would be a long delay before her uncle was of practical help.

After long and anxious consideration, she thought it best to make her appeal to old Mr. Harringay, the doyen of her uncle's tenants; for, since his farm was just beyond the zone of her wanderings, she had never had occasion to ruffle his agricultural or sporting sensibilities. Accordingly, one afternoon she rode up to the Hill Farm where he lived, and found him and his wife taking their tea in the garden. They were very pleased to see her, and she had tea with them. She did not broach the subject of her errand till it was over; it seemed to her that that would not be polite. She talked to them sedately of the affairs of the neighbourhood. Then, when the maid had carried away the tray, she said, "I came to ask you to do something for me, Mr. Harringay."

"I shall be happy to do anything to oblige your ladyship," he said.

The Lady Noggs's face fell, and she said, somewhat ruefully, "It's funny that everybody always says that when I ask them to do something for me; but when they hear what it is, they generally don't do it."

"Well, let's hope it isn't going to be like

that this time," said Mr. Harringay with a twinkling eye. "What is it you want me to do?"

"I wanted to ask you to give William Cotteril work — not a job — regular work."

Mr. Harringay's eyes lost their twinkle, and he said, "Oh, Cotteril — ah, yes — you want me to give him work — regular work. He's a bit of a ne'er-do-weel, isn't he?"

"Oh, no, he isn't!" said the Lady Noggs quickly. "It's only Morton says he is. And he's only trying to pay him out for marrying Liza. He's set every one against William."

"What's that?" said Mrs. Harringay. "I didn't know that Morton had ever been a sweetheart of Liza."

"Oh, he wasn't!" said the Lady Noggs. "He only wanted to be; but Liza wouldn't let him." And she plunged into the story of Morton's attempt to be revenged, and how she had baulked him. They listened to her with the liveliest interest; and when she had told the story, Mrs. Harringay said, "I never did like that Morton. He was always a sulky brute."

"I never liked him either," said Mr. Harringay. "But then I've had several rows with him. He's too domineering. But he seems to have got

the worst of it this time, thanks to your ladyship."

"And you will give William work?" said the
Lady Noggs.

"Yes, certainly, I will give William work, and
if I find him satisfactory I shall say a word to
McNaghten, and tell him that Morton's been
slandering him."

"Oh, thank you!" said the Lady Noggs.
"And may I tell him to come and see you?"

"You may tell him to come this very evening
if you like," said Mr. Harringay.

"I will," said the Lady Noggs.

She was eager to be off with her good news to
the Cotterils; but at the dictates of politeness
she went round the garden with Mrs. Harringay
and admired her roses. Then she thanked Mr.
Harringay again, and rode off. She called at the
cottage of the Cotterils, and told them that William was to go up to see Mr. Harringay, who
would give him work; and she escaped as quickly
as she could from the expression of the gratitude.

Mr. Harringay was as good as his word. He
gave William regular work at once; and it
seemed as though Fortune had satisfied her
spite against the Cotterils, and that now they
were going to enjoy peace after their troubles.

She had not. A few days later the Lady Noggs, who had gone for a ride before lunch, was trotting through the village, when she was dismayed by the sight of the doctor coming out of the Cotterils's cottage door. She trotted on to the gate and cried, "What's the matter, Doctor Hamerton? Who's ill?"

"Mrs. Cotteril's baby. He's swallowed a pin, and it's stuck in his throat," said the doctor; and his cheery face was overcast and gloomy.

"Is he very ill?"

"I'm afraid there's no hope for him. I could get it out if I had the instruments; but I haven't, and I know of none nearer than London. There every hospital has them."

"Then he must go to London!" cried the Lady Noggs.

"It can't be done. I've just worked it out. The pin must be extracted inside of four hours to save him. If we could have caught the Northern Star at Micklefield we could have got him to a hospital in plenty of time. But it's due at Micklefield in twenty minutes; and it's fifteen miles away. No: there's no hope for the poor little soul."

"Oh, what a pity!" said the Lady Noggs with a sob.

"It is a pity; and that confounded express runs through Chandler's Bury — only a mile and a half away!" And with a hopeless gesture the doctor raised his hat, and went on into the village.

The Lady Noggs slipped off Villikins, threw the reins over the gate-post, and went softly in through the open door of the cottage. Mrs. Cotteril sat beside the fire, staring down with dazed eyes at the suffering mite on her lap; William, summoned from the fields, sat just in front of her, all the ruddiness faded out of his face.

"I'm so sorry, Liza," said the Lady Noggs, coming to her and touching her hand; and she looked at the child, which was shaken by a choking little cough, and then moaned.

Mrs. Cotteril's lips moved, but no sound came from them, and her eyes never moved from the little drawn face; but William said thickly, "It's crool 'ard, your ladyship, crool 'ard."

They were silent for a minute or two; and the big tears ran down the cheeks of the Lady Noggs. Then there came again the little choking cough and the moan. The Lady Noggs turned her eyes away from the baby; she could not bear the sight. They wandered round the room, and rested on the red handkerchief knotted round

William's throat. In moments of painful emotion the mind will seize on some trivial object and busy itself with it to get away from the pain. So the mind of the Lady Noggs seized on the red handkerchief, started a relieving train of thought and jumped by a natural association, seeing that she had just been talking of the express, to the red flag of the railway signal man.

Then came an idea so dazzling that she shut her eyes for twenty seconds to grapple with it, opened them, and cried, "I'll stop the Northern Star!"

The Cotterils stared at her bewildered: the sharpness of the cry had roused even Mrs. Cotteril from her stupor; and William said dully, "You'll stop the Northern Star, your ladyship?"

"Yes; I'll stop it in Chandler's Bury! How many of those red handkerchiefs have you?" said the Lady Noggs.

"Three," said William, yet more bewildered.

"Get them quick! We'll make a red flag, and wave it in front of the train and stop it. Then Liza can get into it, and take the baby to a London hospital!"

A dull gleam of understanding shone in William's eyes, and he rose.

"Be quick!" cried the Lady Noggs imperiously. "And — and — take that broomstick to tie them to! Put on your hat, Liza! Be quick!"

Her vehemence carried them away. William stumbled to the chest of drawers, and took out two handkerchiefs. Mrs. Cotteril, a faint flush of hope on her cheeks, got on her hat somehow, and wrapped the baby in a shawl. She was half out of the door when William said, "But what about the money for the tickets?"

"I never thought of that!" said the Lady Noggs, and her face fell. "We can't tell any one, or they'll stop us!"

She stood still, her quick little brain working swiftly; then she cried, "I know! I can get it! You go on to the Bury, and I'll bring it!"

She ran down the path, mounted Villikins, and galloped off towards the castle. The Cotterils stared after her; then William said, "Come on, lass! It's the little un's only chance! Carry 'im soft!" and they set off at a run down the road.

Villikins galloped for all he was worth to the castle stables. The Lady Noggs jumped off him, cried to a groom to hold him, and raced up to the nursery. She took down from the mantel-piece the missionary-box which a misguided aunt had given her in the hope of benefitting her niece and the heathen at one stroke, and looked round the room for something with which to break it open. The poker was too light; the coal-scuttle was empty. Her eyes fell on the soapstone image of Buddha which occupied, inappropriately enough, the place of honour on the mantel-piece beside the missionary-box. She dragged up a chair; mounted on it; lifted down the Buddha; set the missionary-box on the hearth-rug; and banged him down, stern foremost, on to the top of it. There was a crunch and a jingle; she pulled the Buddha off the ruin, dropped on her knees, and with deft fingers sorted out the gold and silver subscribed by her uncle's guests from the copper offerings of humbler friends. She thrust the money into her pocket, bolted down the stairs, and in less than a minute was on the back of Villikins, and galloping for Chandler's Bury.

A quarter of a mile from it she overtook the hurrying Cotterils, and they pressed on together. At the top of the cutting the Lady Noggs dismounted, gave Villikins a cut which sent him galloping home, and they went down to the railway line. The baby seemed no worse for the hasty journey: the little choking cough and moan came no oftener. They sat down a few feet from the line, panting; and William began to knot the handkerchiefs together for the flag. Mrs. Cotteril snatched them out of his trembling, clumsy fingers, and made it herself very quickly. Then, shading her eyes, they started down the line for the train. The minutes dragged.

Presently the Lady Noggs said, "I think I'd better go to London with Liza and the baby, William. I know all about cabs, and I can see they don't lose time."

"Yes, your ladyship," said William; and then, his face working with a new terror, he added, "But suppose they won't let none of you get into the train, stopping it like this?"

"I never thought of that!" cried the Lady Noggs dismayed.

"It's as like as not," said William hoarsely.

The Lady Noggs was silent with knitted brow, striving to find a way to prevent this misfortune. The Cotterils looked at her, open-mouthed, with beseeching eyes, as to an oracle. At last she said, "I was going to wave the flag and stop the train myself, because they wouldn't send me to prison, at least not to an ordinary one. I'm a peeress, you know. But if you stopped the train, William, we might get in on the other side, while the guard and engineer were asking you what's the matter. But they're nearly sure to send you to prison."

"I don't care! I'm game, your ladyship! I'd go to prison for ten year for the little 'un!" said William; his heavy face was transfigured by devotion.

"You might run away when the guard is a good way from his van: the train will have to wait till he gets back to it."

"Never you mind about me, if only you gets the missus an' the little 'un into the train," said William feverishly.

"I will," said the Lady Noggs firmly.

She and Mrs. Cotteril crossed the line, and settled themselves beside a clump of furze which screened them a little. William doggedly pulled off his boots, stood up, and looked down the line. Presently he cried, "There's the smoke!" and began to wave the red flag furiously, though the express was a mile away.

In a minute the Lady Noggs could see the body of the train, and hear its roar; then she distinguished its two engines. The rattling roar grew and grew as it came tearing along; and it seemed as if it must rush past them. But of a sudden there rose a grating squeal from the tortured metals as the brakes locked the wheels, which rose louder and louder and then died down as the train came to a standstill in front of them. It was the work of a moment for the active child to clamber on to the foot-board, and open the door of a first-class compartment. She helped Mrs. Cotteril up and in, and shut the door. The bang made a tall man, who was head and shoulders out of the opposite window, pull himself in. "Sakes alive!" he said.

"Hush! hush!" cried the Lady Noggs, clasping her hands. "Please, don't say anything! The baby's swallowed a pin; and I stopped the train to take it to a London hospital!"

"Jee-rusalem!" said the stranger, dropping into a seat.

The Lady Noggs slipped past him, thrust her head out of the window, cried, "Run, William! Run!" and drew it in again.

William gave a hoarse shout, wrenched the handkerchiefs off the broomstick, flung it from him, and bolted up the steep bank. The guard, who was within thirty yards of him, bolted up after him, but the bootless William gained at every step, and was over the hedge and on level ground with a fifty yards start. The Lady Noggs and the stranger watched the guard gallantly breast the ascent and come to the top. There he stopped suddenly short, and put up his hand to shade his eyes. His head turned this way and that; he shook his fist at the landscape, turned, and came running back. Plainly William had disappeared. The guard reached the bottom just beneath their window; the stranger put his head out of it, and cried, "Hello, conductor, what's the matter?"

"Some — yokel playing a joke!" said the guard, very red with rage and exercise.

"Curious notion of humour yew Britishers hev," drawled the stranger.

"The company'll humour him, when it gets the detective down here," snorted the guard; and he ran along to his van.

"I reckon we've shook *him*," said the stranger, smiling at the Lady Noggs.

"Thank you very much," she said; and her grateful eyes shone on him.

"Say now," said the stranger feasting his eyes on her, "yew flagged an express — a British express?"

"Flagged it?" said the Lady Noggs in some doubt. "Oh, yes; I made William stop it with a flag. I had to. The doctor said it was the only chance of getting the pin out of the baby's throat to take him to a London hospital."

"Sand" — said the stranger, with evident en-joyment — "sand up to the brim. And they told me this decayed old country was played out. Who air yew, young lady?"

"I'm Lady Felicia Grandison."

"Lady Felicia Grandison?" said the stran-ger, and his eyes opened wider. "This beats the Dutch! — a scion of a corrupt and effete aris-tocracy. Wal, travellin' teaches. I'm John P. Cooper, of New York City."

The train started with a little jerk; then the tension suddenly relaxed; and the Lady Noggs threw up her hands over her face, and burst into a fit of tearless sobbing. John Cooper let her sob for three minutes, then he said sharply, "Take a pull, Lady Grandison! Take a pull! Yew've got to look after the youngster!"

The Lady Noggs choked down her sobs, though her mouth went on twitching, and turned to the baby. The stranger moved down to the seat opposite him, and took a careful look at him: "He's powerful sick," he said, "and I've had a sick child of my own, a very sick child. It's my notion that brandy is what he wants. It'll keep him going."

With that he took from his grip-sack a flask of brandy-and-water, poured some on to his little finger, and let a single drop trickle from it into the baby's mouth. He did this at intervals of about two minutes till the baby had had ten drops.

"Seventy-five minutes more," he said, looking at his watch. "He'll do for another hour." And truly the baby's face looked a little less drawn, though the little choking cough and the moan came at the same interval.

They sat watching him in a strained silence, only broken by an occasional question from John Cooper, and the oft-reiterated cry of the Lady Noggs, "Oh, I do wish the train would go quicker!"

In about an hour John Cooper began to give him some more brandy, and the train was running through the suburbs as he finished. "Now," he said, "what about the tickets? I guess we've no time to waste. Micklefield was the last stop before you flagged this excited bathing-machine; and we'll have the money ready."

He took a time-table from his grip-sack, looked up the list of fares, and said, "Sixteen and eightpence." Then he pulled a handful of money from his pocket, and looked at it ruefully: "I don't seem to get ahead with this money of yours," he said.

"Oh, I must pay!" said the Lady Noggs. "William is my uncle's tenant."

John Cooper looked at her earnestly for a minute; then he said, "I reckon that's the feudal spirit, and it's got to be humoured. Have yew got the money?"

"Yes," said the Lady Noggs, pulling it out of her pocket. "I — I broke open my missionary-box."

John Cooper slapped down his hand on his thigh and held it out, saying, "Yew robbed the heathen to play this game? Shake!"

The Lady Noggs shook hands and said, "I had to."

"You bet yew had," said John Cooper.

After some arithmetic the Lady Noggs gave him a sovereign and two half-crowns, the price of a ticket and a half. The train ran into the terminus, and he said cheerfully, "Now it's up to John P. Cooper."

It was: he had them through the crowd, past the ticket-barrier, and into a hansom in eighty seconds; and they were off to the Charing Cross hospital as fast as the horse could get through the traffic. He had them out of the hansom and into the hospital hall before they realized that they had reached it, and was saying to the receiving nurse, "This is Lady Felicia Grandison. She's brought up a tenant's baby with a pin in its throat. If yew're going to put it through, it's got to be done straight!"

His briskness seemed catching, for a smart young house-surgeon and another nurse were on the spot in a moment; he examined the baby, said sharply, "Bring it along quick! Number three!" and hurried on ahead.

The nurse took the baby from Mrs. Cotteril, and then followed her along the corridor to the door of number three. She said, "Wait here, please," went in with the baby and shut the door.

John Cooper made them sit down on a bench in the corridor; and there they waited, the Lady Noggs holding Mrs. Cotteril's hand. Now and again the poor woman said feverishly, "Oh, I hope they won't 'urt 'im! I hope they won't 'urt 'im!" Always John Cooper said cheerily, "Yew bet they won't — no, madam. Not on your life!"

The minutes dragged: it was worse than waiting for the Northern Star. But at last the nurse came out with the baby in her arms.

"It's all right," she said triumphantly. "It's out. Seven minutes: almost a record. I'm taking him up to the children's ward. Come back in an hour. We shall know then how he's stood it."

"God bless your little ladyship!" cried Mrs. Cotteril, and burst out crying and sobbing.

When they had soothed her, she would by no means leave the hospital till she had heard that the baby was out of danger. They left her in the hall; and John Cooper arranged with a nurse that she should have some tea.

Outside the hospital he said, "Yew look as if yew wanted tea, too, Lady Grandison, a square meal."

"Well, I missed my dinner of course," said the Lady Noggs, who was looking a little pale after the strain. "But I mustn't spend much of this missionary money."

"This is my shout," said John Cooper firmly.

They wired to William Cotteril, drove to the Carlton, and over the meal improved their acquaintance at a great rate. By the time they had done, indeed, the Lady Noggs reckoned John Cooper one of her intimate and most amusing friends. When they went back to the hospital, they learned that the baby was doing well after the operation; and the Lady Noggs was taken to see him sleeping in his cot. When she came down she learned that he was to be kept at least three days in the hospital, and that Mrs. Cotteril wanted to stay in London, and a nurse had offered to find her a room near the hospital. At once the Lady Noggs gave her the rest of the missionary money. They bade her good-bye, and left the hospital.

Outside John Cooper said, "Hev you left yourself any money to get home with, Lady Grandison?"

The Lady Noggs thrust her hands into her pocket, drew it out empty, and said with an air of dismay, "Oh dear, I forgot all about that!" Then her face cleared. "But you'll lend it me, won't you?"

"I'm taking you home," said John Cooper. "I'm going to see you to the end of this."

They drove to the station, and there he had time to see to his neglected luggage before they caught the train down to Warlesden. There they were lucky enough to find a fly to drive them to Stonorill. About a mile from the gates of the park they met a group of searchers. In the ordinary course, no notice would have been taken of the absence of the Lady Noggs before eight or nine o'clock at night; but the return of Villikins without a rider had very naturally filled them with the fear that she had met with an accident, and the country had been up, as it was well used to be, hunting for her all the afternoon. William Cotteril, who could have thrown a reassuring light on her disappearance, had returned quietly to his work at the Hill Farm, having recovered his boots from the railway embankment after the Northern Star had continued its interrupted journey; and he had preserved a discreet reticence in the matter of the events which had bereft Stonorill of its young mistress.

The group of searchers having learned that she was safe, dispersed very much in the temper of the shepherds to whom the ingenious but foolish shepherd boy of the fable was in the habit of crying, "Wolf! wolf!" to inform other bands of searchers that their efforts had been misplaced.

The Lady Noggs and Mr. John Cooper drove on and reached the castle before the news of her safety; and, dragging him with her, she rushed into the hall to find the Prime Minister in the middle of an anxious group of his guests concerting measures for a more thorough search.

"Oh, uncle," she cried, "I'm so glad you're not at work! This is Mr. John P. Cooper, of New York City; and he's awfully interested in our old nobility — that's what he calls us. And he'll be so pleased to see you, because you must be a — a — a chief old noble. This is my uncle, Lord Errington, Mr. Cooper; he's Prime Minister."

"Oh, Felicia," groaned the Prime Minister. "What have you been doing? We have been so anxious about you; we thought — "

"Now what's the good of being anxious about me? I always come home some time!" cried the Lady Noggs in a bitterly aggrieved tone. "Somebody's always worrying. How was I to know that Liza's baby would get a pin in its throat, and I should have to flag the Northern Star and take him to London? I hadn't time to tell any one — I hadn't, really."

At this engaging though hardly coherent explanation a chorus of questions rose on the air, and after some confusion she told her tale at length. Some of the Prime Minister's guests applauded her resource and the vigour with which she carried out her plan; others were very properly shocked at the invasion of the sacred rights of the inviolable express, and went on to express a lively apprehension of the action the railway company might take in the matter. The Lady Noggs was entirely defiant; thoughtfully dropping William Cotteril out of the affair, she took the whole responsibility on herself and cried again and again, with greater heat at each repetition, "I had to stop the beastly old train! And I don't care what the silly old railway company does!"

There were some who took the point of view that the railway company is bound to stop the train in a matter of life and death; but, since considerable doubt was expressed as to whether this was really such a case, it was resolved in the end that Mr. Borrodaile should go up to London on the morrow and confer with the officials; and he said sadly: "This time, Noggs, it's a touch and go whether they send you to prison or not. They're rather besotted; and I've told you many times about the pitcher which went to the well too often."

"I don't care!" cried the Lady Noggs joyfully, "I shall go to the Tower — they'll have to send me there, because I'm a peeress — and I shall escape, Billy, you see if I don't!"

"We know you will — we know you will, Noggs," said Mr. Borrodaile. "But the Tower will be anxious, not we."

The Prime Minister had now the leisure to thank John Cooper for the aid he had afforded to his enterprising niece, and would not hear of his returning to town that night. Evening dress was found for him, and he dined and slept at the castle.

In the morning he was up early, and with great enjoyment explored the grounds under the intelligent guidance of the Lady Noggs. After breakfast, under the same intelligent guidance, he explored the castle itself from battlement to basement, showing no less interest in the cost of its up-keep, and the management of the staff of servants, than in the bric-a-brac, the pictures, old furniture, tapestries, and masterpieces of the other arts which adorned it. About noon a wire came from Mrs. Cotteril to tell them that the baby was well again; and it set their minds at rest. After lunch the Lady Noggs drove him to the station in her pony-cart, and, having arranged to meet soon in London, they parted with every expression of mutual regard.

On her way back the Lady Noggs saw in front of her the Rev. Beverley Cringle, the rector of Stonorill, and her face fell, for she foresaw unpleasantness. However, she drove on, resolved to have it over, stopped the pony beside him, and said, "Oh, Mr. Cringle, I've broken open my missionary-box and spent all the money."

The Rev. Beverley Cringle was, not to put too fine a point upon it, a pompous ass. His idle life gave him full leisure to cultivate the petty vanities, and he was very vain of the fact that the missionary-box of the Lady Noggs made Stonorill's contribution to the C.M.S. far greater than those of the neighbouring villages. At this intelligence he pursed up his lips, puffed out his cheeks, and said: "What does this mean? You shock me, Lady Felicia! You shock me!"

"Well, I couldn't help it," said the Lady Noggs. "Mrs. Cotteril's baby had got a pin in its throat; and I had to have money to take it to London at once, or it would have died."

"What?" puffed Mr. Cringle, grown suddenly very like an angry turkey-cock. "Am I to understand that you have wasted the money collected for the heathen on the baby of a common labourer?"

"I didn't waste it. It saved his life," said the Lady Noggs hotly.

"This is shocking — shocking!"

"Well, I knew the baby, and I don't know any heathen."

"That has nothing to do with it — the baby of a ne'er-do-well like William Cotteril! The money must be replaced!"

"Then it just shan't be!" said the Lady Noggs, filled with wrath at the unjust aspersion on her *protege*. "I collected the money and I'll spend it how I like — on charity! And I won't collect any more for the heathen! I'll get a box for sick children!"

"This is worse and worse!" stuttered Mr. Cringle. "Our — our first duty is to the heathen."

The Lady Noggs gave Villikins a cut, and, as he dashed off, she cried: "It can't be! The heathen haven't got pins in their throat — so there!"

The Lady Noggs had the last word.

CHAPTER FIVE

THE LADY NOGGS RECEIVES AN
INVITATION

SOON after her rescue of the Cotteril baby there came a great change in the life of the Lady Noggs. One morning the Prime Minister and Mr. Borrodaile were at work in the library: the Prime Minister was reading his letters; and Mr. Borrodaile was hunting through a volume of his chief's earlier speeches for passages which must not be too flatly contradicted in the speech about to embody the *Volte-face* of that statesman's educational convictions.

Suddenly the Prime Minister cried: "Dear, dear! this is very tiresome!"

"Another defection?" said Mr. Borrodaile cheerfully.

"No," said the Prime Minister frowning. "But the Princess of Meiningen-Schwerin has invited Felicia to live with her little daughter, and be brought up with her."

97

"Poor, dear princess!" said Mr. Borrodaile, with unaffected commiseration. "She's going to see life at last. If Nog — If Lady Felicia does not give her a fresh and deeper insight into the pretty ways of the happy Christian child, I'll — I'll eat my new mashie."

"But why, I ask you, why should she have hit upon Felicia, of all children?" said the Prime Minister.

"Unconscious attraction of unlikes," said Mr. Borrodaile. "Lady Felicia looks eighteenth century, but she isn't. The Meiningen-Schwerins don't look eighteenth century, but they are. Besides, it is an advantage when one of the richest heiresses in England happens to be one's daughter's friend. And if ever it comes to be a question of a higher pension — "And he stopped abruptly.

The Prime Minister frowned.

Mr. Borrodaile sat thoughtful for a minute, then he said, "I wonder how Lady Felicia will take it. It's a pity these invitations are practically commands, for that makes it so difficult to get out of."

The Prime Minister's frown deepened; and he said with spirit: "At any other time I should have refused outright, and settled the matter

once and for all. But I'm very much out of fa-
vour already over owing to this education act,
and you may be sure that this arrangement has
been discussed all over the place. You know how
they hang together. I really don't think I can
refuse."

"It *would* be very awkward just now," said
Mr. Borrodaile.

"You don't — you don't think Felicia will
refuse?" said the Prime Minister, with a note of
almost timorous anxiety in his voice.

"I'm sure she will," said Mr. Borrodaile with
conviction. "But that is a matter you can leave
to Miss Caldecott. She will persuade her."

The Prime Minister sighed heavily, then he
rose, rang the bell, and bade the footman who
answered it ask the Lady Noggs to come to him
in the library. He awaited her coming on the
hearth-rug, pulling his beard with some nervousness; and he awaited it some time, for,
owing to an unfortunate accident, the frock
which the Lady Noggs was wearing was torn,
and she had to put on another. At last she did
come, her brilliant beauty the more vivid for the
air of something very like defiance which flushed
her cheek and brightened her eyes. For she came
expecting to hear that some misdeed or other,

she did not know which, but it might have been any one of many, had come to light; and she was ready for trouble.

In a somewhat halting and uneasy fashion the Prime Minister said, "I have an invitation for you, Felicia. The Princess of Meiningen-Schwerin has written to ask you to go to live with her little daghter at Catford Palace."

"Me!" cried the Lady Noggs with the liveliest disgust. "Me go and live with a princess! I won't do anything so horrid! I'm sure she's a stuffy old thing!"

"Dear, dear!" said the Prime Minister. "That is not the way to speak of a princess."

The Lady Noggs did not retract the description. She looked at the Prime Minister with watchful eyes, and said nothing at all.

The Prime Minister waited for a minute for the retraction which did not come, his eyes wandering timorously the while up and down the Lady Noggs, but never meeting hers; then he said: "Surely you've been taught that the invitations of royalty are commands."

"I don't care!" said the Lady Noggs stubbornly. "They aren't going to command me! I shan't take any notice of it!"

The Prime Minister tugged at his beard, and

looked for help to Mr. Borrodaile, who forthwith plunged his eyes into the volume of
speeches he had before him, and turned the
leaves industriously.

"Surely you wouldn't like to be disloyal?"
said the Prime Minister with trivial artful-
ness.

"How can I be disloyal?" cried the Lady
Noggs in unaffected bewilderment. "This princess isn't the king. Why, she must be German,
with a funny name like that. And what's she got
to do with me?"

The Prime Minister looked helplessly at Mr.
Borrodaile; and Mr. Borrodaile, artful in his
turn, said: "But wouldn't you like to live with a
little girl of your own age, and have her always
to play with?"

"No, I shouldn't! You know I shouldn't. I
don't like little girls — little sillies! You know I
don't. I like grownups. And I like Stonorill. I'm
all right here; and I don't want to go away."

Of a sudden the Prime Minister grew firm and
said: "I'm afraid you'll have to go; and, after
all, the discipline of the Meiningen-Schwerin
household will be good for you."

The Lady Noggs gazed at him for a moment
in speechless indignation; then she changed her

tactics, burst into tears and wailed: "You want to get rid of me! You want to get rid of me!"

"Dear, dear! This is very distressing, and so unreasonable!" said the Prime Minister, shuffling about on the hearth-rug in his exasperation. "I don't want to get rid of you at all, Felicia."

"Oh, yes, you do!" wailed the Lady Noggs; and she sobbed in a most affecting fashion.

"Now, Noggs, don't humbug," said Mr. Borrodaile quietly: he had learned by long experience to distinguish her more frequent diplomatic tears from her very rare real ones.

"Humbug!" cried the Lady Noggs hotly, turning on him. "All right; I'll pay you out for that, Billy! Anyhow, I *won't* go!" And she ran out of the room.

The Prime Minister looked at Mr. Borrodaile with the most distressful eyes. Mr. Borrodaile wiped away a smile, and said with an exceedingly serious face, " I think you had better leave it to Miss Caldecott, sir."

The Prime Mnister said dolefully, "Yes, yes; I will speak to her about it. Felicia is a most difficult child."

"The worst thing about Lady Felicia is that she always has such a painfully exact knowledge of what she wants; and the knowledge is always supported by a firm and active resolve to have it," said Mr. Borrodaile.

"I have grave doubts that this arrangement will prove a success," said the Prime Minister.

"It certainly won't prove a success for the princess," said Mr. Borrodaile. "She is sure to hit up against these prime qualities of Lady Felicia and hurt herself."

They returned to their work, trying with little success to dismiss the matter from their minds: one or the other of them kept reverting to it all the morning. After lunch the Prime Minister sent for Miss Caldecott and said: "I suppose Felicia has told you of the invitation she has received from the Princess of Meiningen-Schwerin?"

"No," said Miss Caldecott, "I have not heard anything about it."

The Prime Minister unfolded the matter to her, and Miss Caldecott's face fell. She had no wish to leave Stonorill, and, though she was careful not to admit to herself that the presence of Mr. Borrodaile had anything to do with this reluctance, and assured herself that it was the natural beauty of the place which made her so loth to go, she was probably wrong. At the same time the prospect of changing the English circle at Stonorill for the German circle at Catford could hardly be alluring to one who knew, as she did, the strenuous etiquette of German court life. However, she assured the Prime Minister that she would bring the Lady Noggs to regard the matter in a reasonable light.

She began by discussing the matter with Mr. Borrodaile, and learned from him exactly how the Prime Minister stood; and that it was advisable that the Lady Noggs should go to the princess. Then she approached her resolute pupil. The line she took — and it was the only line to take, considering the firmness of the Lady Noggs on such questions — was that her refusal to accept the arrangement would injure her uncle. Then she made it yet easier for her to consent by pointing out that there was no harm in making a trial of this new kind of life, that she might after all find it very nice, and, if she were really unhappy with the princess, she would, of course, be allowed to return to Stonorill.

The Lady Noggs heard her out patiently, looking at her with grave and serious eyes and puckered brow. She pondered her words a little while, and then said, with the old-fashioned thoughtfulness she sometimes showed: "Of course, if — it is to help uncle, I've got to do it. But I wish he didn't go in for those nasty politics. Look what a bother they are to him." She sighed, and then went on in a more grudging tone: "But I'm only going to try it. If I can't stand it I shall chuck it — so there!"

Thankful to have prevailed, Miss Caldecott let the idiomatic language pass.

Then began a series of pour-parlers between Stonorill and the house of Meiningen-Schwerin. The Prince and Princess of Meiningen-Schwerin belonged to one of those obscure Anglo-German royal families, so very much more German than Anglo, which have an eternal claim on the gratitude of England for the distinguished services they rendered her by being distantly related to George IV. Some seventy years residence in that grateful country has not impaired the family's eighteenth-century attitude to the rest of the world; and the present heads of it live lapped very comfortably in the traditions of Frederick the Great, and follow his august example in the regulation of their little court.

They were far more highly sensible of the extreme honour they were conferring on the Lady Noggs than any one else concerned, and they held out for their own terms.

There was little difficulty about the matter of
the allowance for the Lady Noggs's mainten-
ance, though they fixed the amount in accordance with their high estimation of the privilege
she was about to enjoy. But out of the distrust
and dislike of everything English, which had remained undiminished in the family since it's
immigration into that grateful country, they
would not hear of Miss Caldecott coming with
the Lady Noggs, nor yet even an English maid.
They declared that the Baroness Pulvermacher,
the governess of the little Princess Wilhelmina,
had their full confidence, and would suffice for
the two children.

They had their way in this matter, chiefly
owing to the support they received from Mr.
Borrodaile. He had been giving the matter his
full consideration, and he had come to the conclusion that he wished the Lady Noggs, or, to
be exact, Miss Caldecott, to return as quickly as
possible to Stonorill; and it seemed to him that
the best way to secure this return was to allow
the Court of Meiningen-Schwerin to have its
Lady Noggs undiluted. If Miss Caldecott were
in charge of her, the royal house would be unlikely to realize the full doubtfulness of the blessing it had drawn on itself for some time, since

she would restrain her charge from the full expression of her interesting personality.

The house of Meiningen-Schwerin was both surprised and gratified at getting its way in this matter so easily: and there was much simple, heartfelt joy in Catford Palace at the prospect of the further inflow of honest English gold. They reckoned without their guest.

It was not easy to impair the high spirits of the Lady Noggs for any length of time; but now and again she suffered from fits of extreme unhappiness at the thought of leaving Stonorill. A few days before her going, Mr. Borrodaile found her in one of these gloomy crises, and at once, with thoughtful kindliness, set about cheering her up.

"Look here, Noggs," he said, "don't you be so miserable. You needn't be gone for long. Your uncle is not a bit keen on your going; and we shall all miss you — we shall know what peace is, and I dare say we shan't like it. Practically, you know, you're only going to Catford Palace on trial; and it's quite possible that the princess might not find you satisfactory, and then she would send you back."

The Lady Noggs dried her eyes with a handkerchief which had suffered many vicissitudes, mostly black; and her face brightened a little as she said, "If I weren't satisfactory, would she really send me back?"

"She would indeed," said Mr. Borrodaile.

"But uncle?" said the Lady Noggs. "Wouldn't it harm him? I mustn't do that."

"Not a bit," said Mr. Borrodaile cheerfully. "He has accepted the invitation, and sent you. What more can he do? If the princess finds you an unsuitable inhabitant of her quiet suburban palace, and too unlucky in the matter of getting into scrapes to make a good companion for her daughter, tha has nothing to do with your uncle. The mistake is the princess's."

The Lady Noggs drew a long-drawn breath, and her eyes shone suddenly with an extraordinary brightness, "I see," she said slowly. "Oh, I'll be so unsatisfactory, I'll see she sends me back all right."

Mr. Borrodaile grinned with a lively appreciation of the excitements in store for the little court at Catford, but he said gravely: "You'll have to be careful, or they'll think you're doing it on purpose to get sent back; and it won't work. Mind you let them down gently, or you'll spoil it."

The Lady Noggs nodded her head sagely and

said: "I'll be careful. I'll let them down gently."
And she went her way cheerfully.

Mr. Borrodaile looked after her and said
softly, under his breath: "Poor, dear princess.
I think she'll learn to leave the Grandison family
alone." Then he smiled a slow, machiavellian
smile.

That afternoon Miss Caldecott perceived that
not only had the Lady Noggs recovered an unbroken serenity, but that Mr. Borrodaile also,
who had of late been apt to wear a gloomy
and perplexed air, had grown quite cheerful
again.

She ought to have been pleased by this improvement in his spirits, but she found herself
quite unable to display any sympathetic joy at
it. She had no wish in the world that he should
perceive this lack of sympathy, but it would
seem that he did. For they were strolling in the
garden after dinner, when he said: "I see that
you're both surprised and disgusted at my being
so cheerful when I must so soon be bereft of the
light of your presence."

Miss Caldecott was taken aback by the suddenness of the onslaught. She gasped and stammered, "I — I'm nothing of the kind!"

"Well, it's natural; and I'm sure you've every

right to be," said Mr. Borrodaile with apologetic suavity.

"Natural? I haven't any such right!" cried Miss Caldecott.

"Every right — every right," said Mr. Borrodaile quickly. "When two people are as close to one another as we are, and they are on the verge of what may be a long separation, it is only natural that they should be depressed, and either has a right to resent the other's not being depressed. I saw that you were depressed; and then I saw that you resented my not being — "

"I did not!" cried Miss Caldecott. "I wasn't and I didn't! Oh, you are — I should like — it's impossible — you're always — " And, leaving these cryptic utterances unfinished, she incontinently bolted for the house.

Mr. Borrodaile turned and followed her slowly. He was so cheerful that he could not refrain from a burst of song from light opera, and his singing was execrable.

CHAPTER SIX

A VARIATION IN THE ART OF POODLE-SHAVING

IN spite of the sense of security induced by Mr. Borrodaile's machiavellian counsel, the Lady Noggs took a tearful farewell of Stonorill. But she was far too proud to show herself ill at ease, much less unhappy, when the Princess of Meiningen-Schwerin received her and her uncle at Catford Palace. She met that good, short, stout lady with all the dignity of the head of the Grandisons. The princess talked for a little while with the Prime Minister on subjects which had nothing whatever to do with his errand; and then she dismissed him with eighteenth-century German curtness. He would have liked to see the Princess Wilhelmina and the Baroness Pulvermacher, but the atmosphere of Frederick the Great prevented him from hinting even at his desire. He kissed the Lady Noggs, made his adieu to the princess, and went.

As the door closed behind him, the Lady Noggs made one step towards it, then pulled herself together and said, in a distinct but trembling voice, "This is only a trial, you know."

The little eyes of the princess opened till they were almost of average size: "A drial? Ach, yes," she said. "But it is not ze coostom to address royal persons vurst. Attend me to ze Baroness Pulvermacher; she vill instrooct you, a drial — ach, yes."

She did not know how much of a trial.

The princess led the way to a little room at the back of the palace, entered, said, "Here is the leedle Englanderin," went out, shut the door, and left the Lady Noggs standing inside it, gazing at her new playfellow and her new governess.

They were hardly an attractive pair: Nature had been kind to neither of them. The Princess Wilhelmina was a strikingly square child. Her figure was square and of considerable amplitude: her face also was square and of considerable amplitude, so that her dot of an upturned nose was but little of a relief to the wide expanse, a very small kopje in a very large veldt. Her eyes were small; and her lips were small and thin. These unattractive features would have mattered nothing at all had they been informed with the right expression; but unfortunately her face gained in ill-humour what it lost in intelligence. As for the Baroness Pulvermacher, Nature had plainly intended her for a Pomeranian Grenadier, and changed her mind at the very last moment, when it was too late for anything to be done.

The governess and pupil stared at the Lady Noggs in a somewhat rude and unamiable fashion. The Lady Noggs surveyed them with an unaffected lack of interest; then the Baroness Pulvermacher croaked, "How do you do, leedle Englanderin?"

"How do you do?" said the Lady Noggs coldly; and she walked to an easy-chair and sat down.

"Ach! Vot ees dat you do?" cried the baroness. "You do not seat yourselfs in de brezence of the Brinzess Wilhelmina till she geef you permizion!"

"I have the right to sit in the presence of the king," said the Lady Noggs, asserting her privilege as head of the family of Grandison.

"Vot ees dat do us? Brinzess Wilhelmina is a Sherman brinzess! Get oop! Get oop! Ad vonce!"

The Lady Noggs sat still and said nothing.

The baroness bounced out of her chair, rushed to her, and dragged her up; the Lady Noggs sank limply to the carpet. The baroness dragged her up again; there was some entanglement of their feet, which the Lady Noggs might have explained, and the baroness sat down on the floor with a violence which shook the room: there was a good deal of her to sit down. The little princess broke into a cackling laughter, for she thought that her governess had hurt herself badly.

The baroness rose with a dazed air, looked at the Lady Noggs, who was sitting once more in the easy-chair, and went thoughtfully back to her seat at the table. From it she gazed at her new charge with dazed eyes.

"I like you," said the Princess Wilhelmina to the Lady Noggs: "You may kizz mine 'and."

"I only kiss the King's hand or the Queen's," said the Lady Noggs ungratefully.

"I dell mamma eef you don't," said the princess.

"Are you a sneak?" said the Lady Noggs coldly.

"Ach, Gott! Ach, Gott! Vot to uz ees going

to 'appen?" panted the baroness. "You veel be vipped, you! You leedle Englanderin!"

"You couldn't do it!" cried the Lady Noggs hotly, flushing. "And if you did, my uncle would take me away at once!"

The baroness glared at her and drummed wildly on the table. The Lady Noggs had found the strong point in her position; the royal house of Meiningen-Schwerin could not lose the Lady Noggs, or rather the allowance; and if her governess were the cause of her going, it was more than likely that the governess would go too.

The Lady Noggs employed the pause in examining the room in which she was for the future to receive instruction; it affected her with no sense of pleasure. The heavy furniture of lustrous mahogany, the heavy curtains, the large but ungainly ornaments, its air of mid-victorian solidity, were in such extravagant contrast to the charming lightness of the decoration of her rooms at Stonorill that they impressed even her child's mind with their insensate heaviness. The baroness still drummed on the table, cudgelling her slow brain for a possible method of dealing with an English peeress, when there came the dull mutter of a distant gong.

It was a welcome diversion. The Princess Wilhelmina slipped heavily out of her chair crying, "Da's loonch! Come along, Englanderin!"

She came round the table, took the arm of the Lady Noggs, and dragged her out of the room and down the stairs. Half-way down she bethought herself to pinch her arm viciously; and on the instant the Lady Noggs retorted with a tug which loosened half the not innumerable hairs in her head.

"Ow! ow! ow!" squealed Wilhelmina. "The Englanderin has bulled mine 'air! Ow! ow! ow!"

The princess, the prince, two ladies-in-waiting, an equerry, and four poodles burst pellmell from the dining-room, and began to console their squealing darling. When the squeals hushed, they turned on the Lady Noggs in furious upbraiding.

"It's all right," the Lady Noggs protested. "She pinched me, and I pulled her hair. It was quite fair."

"Mein Gott!" cried the prince, raising his fat hands to heaven. "Ees eet a leedle teffil ve haf amongsd uz ?"

In time quiet was restored, Wilhelmina's

tears were dried, and they went into the dining-room. The prince and princess, with Wilhelmina between them, sat on one side of the table; on the other sat the four poodles on high nursery chairs; the ladies-in-waiting, the equerry, the Lady Noggs, and the baroness stood on one side in graceful, silent attendance, while the servants fed the royal family, and the royal family fed the poodles. The Lady Noggs soon grew somewhat weary: she could not follow the slow talk of the prince and princess, for they talked in German; the entertainment afforded by their barbarous and noisy fashion of eating soon palled; and she could find no mischief to busy her idle hands. The poodles alone interested her; and she gathered that they were named, in a singular but doubtless complimentary spirit, after the four leading sovereigns of Europe, — Edward, William, Franz Joseph, and Nicolas. At last she grew tired indeed of the royal meal, for it not only seemed interminable, but, as it went on, the atmosphere grew heavier and heavier with the steamy smell of boiled sausage and stuffed poodle.

When the royal family had finished its meal the prince and the princess retired with stately dignity, though their royal air was somewhat spoiled by the flush of repletion. Then their train took its meal, and the Lady Noggs lunched with it. She did not like the food, which, though doubtless of English origin, had become appallingly German in the process of cooking. The conversation was of no interest to her whatever. The Princess Wilhelmina remained with them, and displayed an interesting quality of humour. She employed her leisure in engaging pranks, of which the unfortunate ladies-in-waiting were the victims. She would thump them on the back as they were in the act of drinking, or she would pinch them. She dropped salt down the back of one, and poured water down the back of the other. The conclusion of each pretty trick was followed by little bursts of her cackling childish laughter. Long before the end of the meal the Lady Noggs understood their wary attitude to their food and drink. Wilhelmina left the Lady Noggs severely alone, remembering doubtless the swift and vigorous pulling of her hair.

After lunch the Baroness Pulvermacher and her two pupils returned to the schoolroom. The baroness sat down in an easy-chair, and was at once fast asleep and snoring. Princess Wilhelmina was for going to sleep, too, but of this

the Lady Noggs would not hear. She insisted
on an exploration of the palace and gardens,
but, remembering Mr. Borrodaile's injunction
to let the royal household down lightly, she was
as good as gold all that afternoon.

At tea there was the same attendance on the
royal family and its poodles; and after tea,
since that liquor is not of soporific tendency,
the train remained in attendance. The Lady
Noggs found standing about and saying nothing
exceedingly tedious; and she found the cere-
monies which accompanied the performance of
any trivial action more tedious still. However,
she got through the rest of the day without
any further revelation of her strenuous char-
acter.

At nine o'clock that night she was dismissed
to bed, and never in her life had she gone up to
her bedroom with greater pleasure. The royal
household had taken no pains to make her comfortable, and she regarded the thick and the
thinner feather-beds, between which apparently
she was expected to sleep, with some dismay.
Her trunks, too, half unpacked, since she had
had to get out an evening frock in some haste,
added nothing to the tidiness or pleasantness of
the room. Her first act was to deal with its stuffi-

ness by opening the window, top and bottom, as wide as it would open; then she set about making her toilet. It was all easy but the brushing of her hair, a thing she had never been used to do herself; and it was indeed a difficult and almost impossible task to deal with it properly. Fortunately, in the middle of it, Fraulein Von Reyersbach, one of the princess's ladies-in-waiting, knocked at her door. Out of kindness of heart, she had come in to see if the little strange child was comfortable; and learning her difficulty, she brushed it for her. She was amazed and considerably alarmed by the open window, and adjured the Lady Noggs to shut it, lest the fresh air on a hot night should irreparably damage her health. The Lady Noggs assured her that she was used to fresh air at all hours of the day and night. But again, after saying goodnight, the good-hearted girl begged her not to run this appalling risk.

The Lady Noggs got into bed, and in half a minute threw the thinner, feather-bed which was to cover her, on to the floor; then she composed herself to sleep with some doubt as to the feasibility of slumber in such a remarkably downy nest on such a hot night. She was just dropping off to sleep when the door opened, and the Baroness Pulvermacher blundered in. The sight of the open window drew from her a cry of horror. She saw the golden hope of the house of Meiningen-Schwerin carried off by an attack of pneumonia, and slammed one sash up and the other down with grunts of terror. The Lady Noggs said never a word; but when her door had closed behind the baroness, she locked it. Then she opened the window again.

Fortunately the prince and princess breakfasted in their rooms. Their train, along with the Baroness Pulvermacher and her pupils, breakfasted together. For the first time in her life, the playfulness of the Princess Wilhelmina was checked. She had hit upon the happy idea of jabbing Fraulein Von Reyersbach with her fork. The Lady Noggs said quietly enough, "Don't do that again, Wilhelmina, or I'll smack you."

The Baroness Pulvermacher dropped her knife into her plate with a clatter, flushed with angry horror, and said, "Ees eet dat you give orders to zee Brinzess Wilhelmina, Lady Velicia? Nevare do zo! Nevare!"

Very naturally, on the instant, the Princess Wilhelmina jabbed Fraulein Von Reyersbach again with her fork, and, in the middle of the

cackle of laughter with which she followed up
this humorous effort, the Lady Noggs smartly
slapped her face.

Princess Wilhelmina yelled. The Baroness
Pulvermacher rose and then sank gasping back
in her chair, overcome with surprise and extreme horror. The two ladies-in-waiting looked
at the Lady Noggs with the liveliest consterna-
tion; and the prince's equerry looked at her
with immense surprise tempered by admiration. The Lady Noggs went on quietly with her
breakfast.

When the baroness recovered from the first
shock, she burst into an incoherent storm of reproach and abuse. But since, in the depth of her
emotion, she spoke in German, the Lady Noggs
did not understand a word she was saying, and
went on quietly with her breakfast.

The yells of the Princess Wilhelmina and the
guttural growls of the baroness came to an end
at about the same moment, and the train took
up the interrupted thread of its meal. All except Lady Noggs, from the disjointed fashion
in which they took their food, seemed to have
suffered a severe nervous shock.

After breakfast the children and the baroness
went to the schoolroom, and devoted the morn-

ing to the acquisition of knowledge. After the
interesting and intelligent methods of Miss Caldecott, the Lady Noggs found the teaching of
the Baroness Pulvermacher exceedingly inept.
Neither the prince or princess of Meiningen-
Schwerin was troubled by any new-fangled
ideas about the education of young girls; and,
in the fine old fashion of the Court of Frederick
the Great, Princess Wilhelmina was learning
nothing at all. For an hour the Baroness Pulvermacher growled hoarsely of the glories of the
house of Meiningen-Schwerin, and of the grovel-
ling respect due to her distinguished pupil from
the rest of the world. For another hour she
growled with undiminished hoarseness of etiquette. For an hour she growled of the arts of
reading and writing, in which branches of polite
learning Princess Wilhelmina was about as far
advanced as a bricklayer's daughter at the age
of seven. The Lady Noggs, in spite of the reproaches of the baroness, yawned and yawned.
She was bored to extinction. As the day advanced her boredom grew and grew. Her spirit
chafed at the tedious and absurd etiquette which
was the savour of life to the prince and princess.
It chafed at the needless and intolerable dull-
ness of it all; and it chafed at the appalling

stuffiness of the palace. And when, after tea, she was bidden play with the Princess Wilhelmina, she found her the stupidest playmate that ever irritated an intelligent child. When at last the long day came to an end, she made up her mind that she had done all the letting down gently she possibly could, and that on the morrow she would begin to be firm and unsatisfactory.

Accordingly, the troubles of the house of Meiningen-Schwerin began early. The Lady Noggs was up with the sun or thereabouts, and, by dint of considerable firmness and perseverance, she got her royal playmate out of bed and into the garden. When the two children came in to breakfast, at which both the prince and princess were, unfortunately for their peace of mind, present, the Lady Noggs was in a state of spotless cleanliness; but the hapless Princess Wilhelmina had apparently had a difference with a duck-pond. She was wet to the waist, brown with mud, and green with duck-weed. The outcry rose to the skies: the prince and princess, the baroness, and the ladies-in-waiting were all expressing their loud horror and dismay togethe to an accompaniment of the joyous yelping of the poodles, who foolishly supposed it a new kind of game. The Princess

Wilhelmina protested that they had but been gathering water-lilies and she had fallen in; the Lady Noggs cried, with an anguished plaintiveness, "How could I keep her out of the pond? She's such a silly little girl."

"Seely! seely, mine Wilhelmina? A brinzess of ze blood royal seely?" cried the prince. "Ees eet a barbarian child we haf amongsd uz?"

Breakfast waited while the Princess Wilhelmina was cleaned and redressed; then, with its train in attendance and its poodles at table, the royal family began its meal. In the middle of it the Baroness Pulvermacher was observed to be struggling frantically to pluck the Lady Noggs from a chair on which she was firmly seated; and there followed a wrangle about the privilege of the head of the Grandison family, which left the prince and princess crimson with wounded vanity. Later in the meal they were terrified out of their wits by their little daughter's strenuous efforts to choke herself with her coffee, an effort induced, as she explained, by the agreeable but curious face the Lady Noggs made at her while she was drinking. Once more the torrent of royal wrath swept fruitlessly round that sturdy British rock; and the Royal

House rose from its breakfast unbecomingly heated.

In the schoolroom the baroness, tired of her yawns, told the Lady Noggs to write a nice letter to her uncle, and was agreeably surprised by the briskness with which she set about it. At the end of her harangue on etiquette she looked up, to see that the Lady Noggs had finished the letter and was closing the envelope. She reached forward quickly, took it from her hand, and began to open it carefully, so as not to waste the envelope.

"You're not going to read my letter!" cried the Lady Noggs, opening her eyes wide in her surprise.

"Ach, and why not?" said the baroness in equal surprise.

"Letters are private."

The baroness smiled disdainfully. "Nod ze ledders of leedle girls."

"It's dishonourable!" said the Lady Noggs curtly.

The baroness scowled and flushed: "Ach, you do von vipping vant!" she said with fervent conviction.

She took the letter gingerly from the envelope and read:—

DARLING UNCLE,—I miss you very much. These people are pigs, they are really : you should hear them eat. They talk with their mouthsfull, and Vilhellmeena is the silliest little girl you ever saw. I cannot make her play sensibbly, and I could not help her falling into the pond. Give my love to Billy and Japp, there is only poodles here.

Your loving niece

NOGGS.

The baroness rose gasping, with a very red face, and hurried off to the princess for instructions. The Lady Noggs scowled after her; then her face cleared, and, she said quickly, "I don't like these plain red table-cloths, do you ? Let's make patterns on it with the ink."

When the baroness returned with the letter in fragments, the Princess Wilhelmina was immersed in this entrancing occupation; incidentally she had made patterns on her frock, her hands, her face, and her hair. The Lady Noggs, though her fingers itched to take their share in the joyous task, had wisely confined herself to superintending her efforts, and was of an irritating spotlessness.

The baroness fairly yelled at the sight of her piebald charge; and, after she had had her cleaned, she sat for the rest of the morning with her eyes fixed on the Lady Noggs in an unwavering watch, breathing heavily through the nose. Half an hour before lunch, however, her vocation of secretary to the prince interrupted her vigilance: she was summoned to him to write letters.

As the door closed behind her, Princess Wilhelmina cried joyously, "To-day ees ze day of ze shaving of ze poodles. Ze man ees here now. Coom, led uz go and zee eet."

The eyes of the Lady Noggs brightened with equal joy. "Coom on!" she said; and they hurried upstairs to see the process. They watched it for some time with extraordinary pleasure, asking many questions. Then the poodle-shaver was summoned away to his dinner with the servants, and the children were left alone with the incomplete dogs.

The Lady Noggs, very naturally, had a pair of clippers in her hand before the door closed behind the poodle-shaver, and was working the handles with a cold, calculating eye on the frisking pets. "I don't see the use of all those top-knots and ruffs," she said slowly. "I'm sure they'd look much nicer plain — not so foreign, you know."

"Yez; vouldn't zey?" said Princess Wilhelmina.

The intelligent animals trotted into the dining-room in
a body

"We might clip one and see," said the Lady Noggs, working the clippers.

"Oh, led'z!" said Princess Wilhelmina.

"The requests of royalty are commands," said the Lady Noggs with a quaint smile.

There were two pairs of clippers; one dog led to another; and in eight crowded minutes of glorious life the happy children clipped every vestige of wool off their amiable dumb friends; they had them barer than shorn sheep.

They were smiling happily at one another over their completed work, when the gong for lunch sounded, and the poodles ran to the door. The children put back the clippers among the rest of the poodle-shaver's instruments, swept the shorn wool neatly together, opened the door, and ran downstairs on the heels of the poodles.

The intelligent animals trotted into the dining-room in a body. At the sight of them the pleasant smiles of appetite froze on the large, round faces of the prince and princess, and the mouths of their train opened.

With an anguished cry of "Mine anchels! Mine poor anchels!" the princess sank back gasping.

The prince spat half a dozen z's, and clutched at his collar with every symptom of imminent apoplexy.

"We thought they'd look better plain," said the Lady Noggs in pretty, shy apology.

Their ladies and gentlemen sprang to the aid of the prince and princess; smelling-salts were applied to her; his well-rounded neck was freed from the collar.

When the tumult of the helpers died down, the prince sat staring stonily at his bare favourites, but the princess, with a splendid effort, got to her feet, tottered across the room, and boxed feebly at the Lady Noggs's ears. Her hand only struck a very sharp elbow.

None the less, the Lady Noggs flamed to a fury and cried, "How dare you?"

"Begone! begone!" cried the princess, pointing to the door.

"Dake her away! dake her away!" groaned the prince.

The Lady Noggs gave herself a little shake and stood invested with all the Grandison dignity. "I'm going," she said in a clear voice. "And I'm glad to go. I don't want to stay with dishonourable foreigners who read other people's letters and eat like pigs."

The silence of blank horror fell on the little court as she went out of the room, and carefully shut the door.

CHAPTER SEVEN

THE LADY NOGGS RETURNS

M R. BORRODAILE'S statement, that
when the Lady Noggs had departed
to Catford Palace the dwellers at
Stonorill would know what peace was, proved
true enough. But his doubt that they would
enjoy that blessing, when they obtained it,
proved no less well-founded. Out of the whole
of any given day, the Lady Noggs had been
with them but a short time, yet that short time
had exercised a brightening influence on the
rest of the twenty-four hours; the abiding sense
that she was at hand and probably active, active in some more or less baleful fashion, had
added a spice of exciting uncertainty to their
lives, and now that she had gone they turned
very dull. In the case of Mr. Borrodaile that
dulness was increased a thousandfold by the
fact that the absence of the Lady Noggs was
accompanied by the absence of Miss Caldecott;

and he was awaiting with far greater eagerness than any one else news from Catford. He alone, however, had the very sure expectation that the news would be that the Lady Noggs had proved unsatisfactory.

On the afternoon of the fourth day he sat at tea on the lawn with the Prime Ministèr, and both of them were finding that meal, ungraced by the presence of the Lady Noggs and Miss Caldecott, a somewhat dispiriting affair. They had been together all the day, working hard most of the time, and they were unconsciously resolved to put their work behind them. Unfortunately, this resolve brought it about that they could find nothing to talk about; and they sat smoking their cigarettes in a dull silence.

The rumble of a carriage broke in upon it, and they turned their eyes with a really interested expectation towards the point at which the shrubberies end, and the drive runs unscreened along the edge of the lawn. Presently the carriage rumbled into sight, and proved to be a ramshackle, lumbering fly of the kind which waits dingily about a country railway station. Its roof was loaded with trunks; and at the sight of them a smile of touching content brightened Mr. Borrodaile's face.

The eyes of the Prime Minister rested on those trunks fully two minutes before he exclaimed, in a tone of startled anguish, "Surely those are Felicia's trunks!"

"They are indeed," said Mr. Borrodaile; and his tone was free from any trace of surprise, which was the less remarkable, seeing that he felt none.

"Dear, dear! This is very tiresome!" said the Prime Minister. "The princess must have sent her back. Whatever can have happened?" And he rose hastily.

"The pretty ways of a happy Christian child have happened, plainly enough," muttered Mr. Borrodaile.

The Prime Minister walked swiftly towards the castle, followed by Mr. Borrodaile, and reached its entrance just as the fly disgorged the Lady Noggs and a large, round lady of a singularly gnarled countenance. The Lady Noggs presented an almost ideal picture of calmness and self-possession as she gazed around the familiar scene with a smiling contentment.

The Prime Minister had only time to observe that the large, round lady was flushed and almost stertorous, so heavily was she breathing, when his niece was embracing him with that extravagant show of affection which is not infrequently the effect of a consciousness of guilt in the womanly heart.

The Prime Minister returned her embrace in a distinctly perfunctory fashion, and said in a tone of anxious disquiet, "Why have you come back? What does this mean?"

The Lady Noggs began, in a voice of plaintive protest, "I didn't ask to come back. The princess sent — "

"I am ze Baroness Pulvermacher," broke in the large, round lady with heated vehemence. "And zees ees what it mean! Zat ees von barbarian child! Von leedle savage! She haf shaved ze poodles of ze brincess of every 'air! Zare ees not von 'air left! No, not von 'air!"

The Prime Minister regarded the large, vociferous lady with utter bewilderment. He did not understand one word of this earnest and heated explanation. But he was dimly aware that his niece had distinguished herself in a fashion to which, with every opportunity of doing so, he had never grown used; and he said, "Dear, dear! This is very tiresome! What has happened? I don't understand!"

The Lady Noggs turned on the baroness with

a triumphant air and cried, "There! You see what comes of interfering with people's letters! If you hadn't read my letter dishonourably and torn it up, uncle would have known about the poodles. Now he doesn't!"

"She haf shaved ze poodles — ze poodles of ze brinzess!" cried the Baroness Pulvermacher with yet more heat, making her meaning clearer by rapping the palm of her left hand with the first and middle fingers of the right, and nodding her head with vigour and rapidity.

The Prime Minister looked at her in even greater bewilderment and said, "But you do shave poodles."

"But she haf shaved ze tob-knods and ze ruffs. Zare ees not von 'air! No, not von!"

The Prime Minister gripped his beard firmly, and held on to it.

"And zat ees nod all!" the baroness went on. "She haf flung ze Brinzess Wilhelmina into ze pond! She haf inked her dress!"

"That's a wicked story! Both are wicked stories!" cried the Lady Noggs with a vast and righteous indignation. "The silly little girl did both herself!"

"Vonce more — vonce more," cried the baroness, in the last accents of horror and de-

spair, " she haf called ze Brinzess Wilhelmina
a seely leedle girl!"

"Perhaps, if Lady Felicia would give her version of these interesting occurrences, we should
be able to form a more accurate idea of what has
happened," said Mr. Borrodaile, taking advantage of the fact that the violence of her emotion
had reduced the baroness to a passing silence.

"It was not my fault, except, of course, about
the poodles. And really they did *not* look so
foreign," said the Lady Noggs, voluble but
hardly lucid. "Princess Wilhelmina was gathering water-lilies, and she fell into the pond quite
all herself. Anybody might. And I didn't ink her.
She inked herself. She was only making black
patterns on the table-cloth. The table-cloth was
red."

"An admirable reason," said Mr. Borrodaile.
"But am I wrong in supposing that you were
present when these misfortunes befell your little
playmate?"

"Playmate!" cried the Lady Noggs with infinite scorn. "You should have seen her play!
She didn't know how!"

"But were you present when these misfortunes befell her?" said Mr. Borrodaile, keeping
to his point.

"Yes, of course I was there. Where else should I be?" said the Lady Noggs. "But I didn't ink her. She inked herself. And I didn't throw her into the pond. She fell in. It's a wicked story to say I did."

"And about the poodles?" said Mr. Borrodaile, pursuing the inquiry. "What happened to those intelligent creatures?"

The Lady Noggs's face cleared, and she smiled, as one calling to mind an agreeable and entertaining incident. "Well, they did look rather funny," she admitted. "But how was I to know how they'd look? Any one would have thought they'd have looked better without all those frills and things; and so we clipped them. But they didn't, stupid things! They looked very funny." And she smiled again at the agreeable picture in her mind.

"And zay are ze favoureetes of ze brince and brincess. Zere ees not von 'air left!" said the baroness, taking up once more the burden of her lament with a tearful and moving solemnity.

Mr. Borrodaile suddenly saw a picture of the shorn pets, and he laughed gently. The Prime Minister looked from the Baroness Pulvermacher to the Lady Noggs, and from the Lady

Noggs to the Baroness Pulvermacher, with the unhappiest air.

"What happened then?" said Mr. Borrodaile.

"Oh, then — then the princess was very angry," said the Lady Noggs. "Just as if it was my fault. How was I to know the poodles would look so funny when they were shaved all over? And she told me to go, and tried to hit me. And I was very angry. And I think I was rather rude. But she'd no business to try to hit me."

"She vas insolent! Oh, insolent!" cried the baroness. And she waved her hands with an air.

The Lady Noggs looked at the baroness with utter contempt, and murmured under her breath: "Sneak!"

"You were rude?" said Mr. Borrodaile.

"I only said I was glad to come away, because they were dishonourable people, and eat like pigs. And they are — they read a letter of mine to you, uncle; and then she tore it up. And they do eat like pigs," said the Lady Noggs firmly.

"Dear, dear! This is very tiresome!" said the Prime Minister. "How many times am I to tell you, Felicia, not to call your elders — But there, it is useless talking to you. If you would come with me, Baroness Pulvermacher, we can discuss the matter, and perhaps, uninterrupted, I shall be able to learn something of what has taken place."

With that, he and the baroness went into the castle.

As they disappeared, the Lady Noggs made a bee-line for the tea-table on the lawn, attended by Mr. Borrodaile. His curiosity about the effect of the Lady Noggs on German royalty was by no means sated. The Lady Noggs fell on the thin bread-and-butter with some appearance of voracity; and he said, "You seem hungry."

"I am hungry," said the Lady Noggs. "I could not eat in that palace. You can't eat in a stuffy hole, you know, not even if the food is nice. And it wasn't. I think it must have been German. It never had a clean taste; it was always thick-tasting and greasy."

Mr. Borrodaile plied her with cake and milk and cream; and when she had satisfied her hunger, she sat back in her chair and said: "I *am* glad to be back. You've no notion how beastly it was, Billy — always one's best behaviour."

"You're best behaviour?" said Mr. Borrodaile. "Yes; it won't stand any great strain."

The Lady Noggs sat up very straight in her

chair, and looked at him with extreme suspicion. "What do you mean?" she said. "My best behaviour is very good behaviour."

"Oh, yes, of course — yes, yes," said Mr. Borrodaile hurriedly. "Excellent! excellent!"

The Lady Noggs sank back into an easier posture, and plunged into a bitterly scornful account of the tradition of etiquette which had come down through the years from Frederick the Great to Catford.

Little by little, by dint of questions, Mr. Borrodaile drew from her an unvarnished and disjointed narrative of the events of her three days' stay in the household of Meiningen-Schwerin. To all seeming, he found the tale an entertaining one, for his face was wreathed with smiles all through it; and he laughed gently several times. At the end of it the Lady Noggs said with some anxiety, "I don't think I did anything particularly bad, do you, Billy? Of course, those poodles looked very funny, but I didn't really hurt them, you know."

"No," said Mr. Borrodaile, with his most judicial air. "I don't think you did do anything very bad. The only thing was, that you were a very large pebble to fall into such a quiet little pool."

The Lady Noggs looked at him seriously,

weighing his words; then she said, "It was something like that. What I like about you, Billy, is, you understand things. And, after all, I never wanted to go there." She paused and again reflected; then she said with extreme thoughtfulness: "I think — I think I'll go and look at the animals. If uncle comes straight from that horrid old baroness, he'll have quite a wrong idea of things, don't you know?"

"I think it would be well," said Mr. Borrodaile; and the Lady Noggs strolled off in the direction of the stables, to look at her pets.

Mr. Borrodaile sat still, and lighted another cigarette. Twice he smiled with extreme content, for he looked for the return of Miss Caldecott within the next twenty-four hours. He had finished the cigarette he was smoking, and was half way through another, when the carriage came round to the entrance of the castle; the Prime Minister put the Baroness Pulvermacher into it, and, when she had been borne away, came hastily down the lawn towards him. As he drew near, Mr. Borrodaile saw that his usual harried air was more harried than ever. He sank down in a chair and cried, "Felicia has been behaving shockingly — abominably!"

"Not a bit of it," said Mr. Borrodaile quietly.

"How — what? But she has," said the Prime Minister. "She has not only been mischievous, but positively impudent. She threw the Princess Wilhelmina into a pond; she splashed her with ink; and she pulled her hair in the most painful fashion. Besides, she was most insolent, not only to the Baroness Pulvermacher, but to the prince and princess themselves."

"The Baroness Pulvermacher appears to have unburdened her soul," said Mr. Borrodaile.

"Yes, she's been quite frank and open in the matter."

"Well, for my part," said Mr. Borrodaile, "I don't lay much weight on her frank openness. I prefer Lady Felicia's version of what happened. We know that she tells the truth; and we have no reason to believe that telling the truth is a German habit. I have very little doubt, indeed, that the Lady Felicia is responsible for the misfortunes which befell the Princess Wilhelmina; but I am quite sure that she was not the active agent in bringing them upon that child's luckless head. She did not throw her into the pond. She suggested to her to pluck the water-lilies which grew in it. I admit that the result would be practically the same; but there is a great difference between throwing a person into a pond and suggesting plucking the water-lilies. Again, she told me, and I believe her, that she did not throw ink on her little playmate. She only suggested to her that a black pattern would be a vast improvement to a plain red table-cloth. And all the inking that was done, the Princess Wilhelmina did herself. In the matter of the poodles, she pleaded guilty. But, after all, she did not hurt the dogs. And if people will leave children alone with poodles, and clippers, and ponds, and ink, they can only expect such results. They insisted, with untiring pertinacity, on having their Lady Felicia undiluted; and they've only themselves to blame that she proved too strong for them. Had Miss Caldecott gone with her, as you proposed, there would have been none of this trouble."

As Mr. Borrodaile straightened things out, the face of the Prime Minister slowly cleared. "What you tell me does put a very different complexion on the affair," he said. "But I do wish she had not been so insolent to the prince and princess."

"It hardly seems to have been unprovoked," said Mr. Borrodaile. "Apparently, the princess lost her temper at the sight of the shorn poodles, and tried to box Nog — Lady Felicia's ears."

"Well," said the Prime Minister, "the sooner Miss Caldecott comes back, the better. You have her address? I hope she'll be able to come back at once."

"Since she's staying with that impossible uncle of hers, the South American millionaire, I should think she'd be glad of an excuse to get away."

"Ah, yes; Beresford Caldecott. A terrible person!" said the Prime Minister. "You'd better wire to her at once. Don't let's have any delay. In the meantime, till she comes, I will keep an eye on Lady Felicia myself." He said this in all seriousness, as if he honestly believed the task within the range of his powers.

To divert attention from the smile he could not restrain, Mr. Borrodaile rose hastily and said: "I'll wire at once." And he went off briskly to the house.

The Prime Minister leant back in his chair and sighed. His interview with the infuriated and unintelligible Baroness Pulvermacher had once more set his scrupulous conscience to work to annoy him in the matter of the Lady Noggs. Once more he was pondering the question, whether he was really the kind of man to bring up a little girl, quite unaware of the fact that he had really very little indeed to do with that bringing up.

Presently, accompanied by a guinea-pig, she broke in upon his uneasy meditations. She sat down in a chair facing him, and said: "I'm awfully glad to be back. It was horrid in that stuffy palace. I should think they never opened the windows all the year round; and they tried to stop me having my bedroom window open. They said I should catch cold. Did you ever hear of anything so silly? Aren't you glad I've come back?"

"Yes," said the Prime Minister, with no exaggerated warmth of welcome in his tone. "But I wish you hadn't been insolent to the princess."

"Well, I didn't want to be insolent to her. I never meant to be at all; but when she hit me, I couldn't help it; I couldn't really. And after all it was dishonourable to read my letter, you know. Very dishonourable. And they did eat like pigs. They did, truly."

"Still, I think you'd better write her a nice letter, and explain that you did not mean to be insolent."

"All right," said the Lady Noggs with utter indifference. "I'll write and explain. I have got away from the horrid place anyhow."

In the meanwhile Mr. Borrodaile had written
and dispatched the following telegram:—

Noggs has come back. We are helpless. Lord Errington
begs you to come to our aid as soon as you possibly can.

He was pleased with the wire, and he felt sure
that it was worded strongly enough to give Miss
Caldecott the excuse she must be needing so
badly to escape at once from her uncle's roof.
Beresford Caldecott enjoyed the unchallenged
reputation of being the worst-tempered man in
Europe; and only a somewhat insistent sense of
duty ever brought his niece to his house. As a
rule, that sense of duty could not keep her in
it for more than a fortnight at a time.

Having dispatched the telegram, Mr. Borrodaile thought it well to strengthen his plea for aid
by a letter; and he sat down to write it with extreme pleasure. It is less satisfactory to write
than to talk to the object of one's respectful admiration, but it is better than nothing at all.

The letter was not easy to write, because,
though he had never made any secret of his admiration, Miss Caldecott had always eluded or
checked his attempts to express it. Accomplished
writer of difficult diplomatic letters as he was, he

wrote this one four times before he got it to his liking. At last he finished it, and it ran:—

Dear Miss Caldecott,—

The four weeks of your absence (she had been away exactly four days), and that of your amiable and accomplished pupil, have turned the inhabitants of Stonorill into a dreary, mopey crew. Our spirits are indeed quite broken, and there seems but very little chance of their ever recovering the elasticity which your presence and that of your amiable and accomplished pupil imparts to them. Upon us, in this nerveless and broken condition, there has suddenly descended your pupil, returned, with an unseemly haste, for which I, at any rate, am exceedingly thankful, by the Princess of Meiningen-Schwerin. In our depressed condition we are quite unable to cope with her, the more so as she has returned with a lurid reputation for imponding and inking the young of princes, and of shaving their poodles. We feel that, unless you come to restrain her, our lot will be indeed hapless. Lord Errington therefore begs me to adjure you to come to our help as soon as you can; and, for my own part, I shall count the minutes till your return.

Yours,
William Borrodaile.

For all that Miss Caldecott was looking for a letter from Mr. Borrodaile, the sight of his handwriting on the envelope sent a thrill through her. The thrill surprised and annoyed her; it even disquieted her. She had come, by degrees, to take pleasure in Mr. Borrodaile's never hidden admiration of her, but she had never regarded it seriously: to do so would have been absurd, for it was well understood among his friends that he was to marry a rich wife, whose money would further his ambitions. A marriage with a penniless girl like herself meant the ruin of a career which promised to be so brilliant.

She had been under the impression that she regarded him merely as the pleasantest and most entertaining of her friends. The thrill came as a most unpleasant warning that her deeper feelings might be very much more concerned in the matter than she supposed. At once she resolved not to return to Stonorill for at least a fortnight; and she began also to consider the resignation of her post of governess to the Lady Noggs.

She did not look forward to staying another fortnight with Beresford Caldecott with any pleasure at all. It was seldom, indeed, that a meal in the gorgeous palace he had built for himself passed without her being jarred by the crash of broken crockery; and the fact that there was a perpetual procession of servants through the house, since not one of them who came into contact in any way with its master stayed more than a week, added nothing to the comfort of existence.

His outbursts of rage did not frighten her any longer, but she still found them annoying; and there was something tiresome about his reiteration of the fact that she never need look for a penny of his.

She did not, however, carry out her intention of spending a fortnight with him. Mr. Borrodaile was resolved to get her back to Stonorill with no delay; and he left no means untried to compass that end. He was somewhat doubtful about the effect of his letter. He suggested, therefore, to the Prime Minister that he also should write to her; and since, when actually confronted with the appalling task of keeping an eye upon the Lady Noggs, his heart had failed him, he accepted the suggestion with eagerness, and wrote at once. His letter reached Miss Caldecott the morning after that on which Mr. Borrodaile's had come. She had a great, liking for the Prime Minister, and she knew that his anxiety about the Lady Noggs was never at rest, and she gathered clearly from the letter that it was at the moment acute. After some debate with herself she gave up her intention of staying away from Stonorill for a fortnight, and wired that she would be there that afternoon.

Her uncle greeted the news of her early departure with an outburst of fury: but since he would have greeted the news that she proposed to stay a fortnight, or any other kind of news, with a like outburst, that was neither here nor there. He did not lose the opportunity of once more assuring her that she would never get a penny from him.

On the journey, in spite of her strenuous efforts to keep it out of her mind, the memory of the thrill she had felt at the sight of Mr. Borrodaile's handwriting was somewhat importunate and troubling, until she found herself looking forward to meeting him with something like nervous trepidation. That trepidation was justified by the fact that the sight of Mr. Borrodaile himself, waiting for her in one of the Stonorill motor-cars, sent an even more violent thrill through her than the sight of his handwriting had done.

After that, it was only natural that her greeting should be of a freezing coldness, and that she should show no pleasure at all at being back at Stonorill. Mr. Borrodaile was by no means blind to her coldness, but he did not show his disappointment; with his natural, happy knack of aggravating, he began at once to talk as if she were overjoyed at having returned.

CHAPTER EIGHT

THE LADY NOGGS FINDS A NEW FRIEND

IT really seemed as if the hasty summoning of Miss Caldecott back to Stonorill had not really been needful; as if the unaided eye of the Prime Minister would have been powerful enough to restrain the Lady Noggs from upheaving the peaceful lives around her, so good was she for some time after her brief, meteorlike course through the hearts and home of the royal house of Meiningen-Schwerin.

If she was good, so was Mr. Borrodaile. He did not make any show of his admiration for Miss Caldecott, or, to be exact, he made no more show of it than he had done before she went away.

She was beyond measure relieved by his quietude. Since she found his admiration very pleasant, she persuaded herself with the less difficulty that there was no need to take it seriously, no need ever again to feel any thrill at the sight either of himself or his handwriting. She quite overlooked the interesting psychological fact that thrills are hardly under the direction of the human reason or the human will. Assuredly, it never occurred to her that Mr. Borrodaile, with the machiavelian shrewdness of an accomplished diplomat, might be biding his time, making himself more and more a necessary part of her life until the time came when she should find it hard indeed to do without him. Possibly this course of action was not very clearly defined in his mind. He may have been following it by instinct, only aware that it behooved him to make his approaches slowly and with caution. Be that as it may, after showing herself cold and firmly disposed to fall in with none of his suggestions for a few days, she suffered him to take up again his old, jesting intimacy with her.

It was one of those delightful summer mornings when a light haze blurring the landscape promises a glorious sunny day. The Lady Noggs came upstairs, after breakfasting with her uncle, in a profound self-satisfaction, induced by the fact that she had behaved to him with a nice consideration, and cheered his meal with many profound and judicious observations on the

European situation, which she had heard Mr. Borrodaile discussing with a political guest the night before.

She pulled off the decorative frock, so harmonious with her vivid beauty, in which she had breakfasted, and was arraying herself in a more severe and workmanlike garb of dark blue linen, when the summer air wafted in through the window all the scents of the distant wood. She stopped short in her robing, went to the window, looked out and sighed. The air seemed to her to be teeming with invitations to forsake the house for the open country. She looked slowly round the woods and meadows and her eyes shone with a sudden light. She turned and looked at the clock. It wanted seven minutes to ten, the hour at which her lessons began. With hasty fingers she finished fastening her frock, snatched up a straw hat from the bed, and, holding it low down against her frock, walked out of the room and down the stairs with a look of singular and if anything exaggerated innocence in her limpid eyes.

She met no one but Mr. Borrodaile. At the sight of her excessive innocence his eyes grew alert; then he saw the hat in her hand, and a look of understanding filled his face. The inno-

cence and the hat in conjunction meant truancy. He opened his mouth to turn her from
her purpose by a timely rebuke, then shut it
quickly. The prospect of a pleasant hour or two
in the woods with Miss Caldecott, hunting for
her vanished charge, opened before his mental
vision. He passed the Lady Noggs without a
word.

She slipped out of the side door into the shrubberies, and with flying skirts and streaming hair
raced for the wood. Once in its cool shelter, she
slackened her pace to a saunter, and, fanning
herself with her hat, began to enjoy her freedom.

She went slowly and very softly along the
paths which led to the wood's heart, stopping
many times to watch the doings of its furred
and feathered inhabitants, — a dispute between
a jay and some finches, the young rabbits playing
in the drives, the gambols of families of squirrels in the tree-tops; enjoying the while the
scented air, the dull, pervasive hum of insects,
and the singing of the birds. She wandered
right through the wood, and was passing along
the edge of it where it borders on the meadows
which stretch between it and Stonorill village,
when she heard voices of children on the other
side of the hedge. The quality of them struck

her at once. They were not the low, drawling voices of the Stonorill children, but high-pitched and twanging; and she knew that she was listening to some of the slum children from London who are sent down every summer by some charitable society, and lodge in the cottages of the Stonorill villagers.

She walked to the hedge, and looked through a hole in it down upon four little girls and two little boys. Five of them were gathered into a group, regarding, with eyes in which hostility and contempt were very evenly blended, the sixth, a little red-haired girl in a ragged frock of a colour impossible to be described, since it had suffered so many blurring vicissitudes. Perhaps it was more of the hue of street mud than of anything else. As the Lady Noggs looked down on them, another little girl, in a thick frock of a hot crimson, very distressing to the eye in the summer heat, was, to all seeming, summing up a discussion.

"Git awye!" she cried in an angry, strident voice. "We don't want the likes of you plying wiv us! A low common kid in a hold dirty rag like that! We don't want yer, and we hain't agoing ter 'ave yer! You tike it strite from me!"

With that, the superior five turned their backs on the red-haired pariah, and went off in a body, muttering fiercely among themselves.

The little red-haired girl looked after them wistfully without a word. She gave her eyes a sharp rub with grimy knuckles, then looked down at the turf with the unrepining resignation of a person inured to Fortune's cruelties. She kicked idly at a tuft of grass with a boot several sizes too large for her and split across the toe.

The Lady Noggs, ignorant of the social hierarchy and of the vast gap between the classes in which the child in the crimson frock and the little red-haired girl respectively moved, was indignant at the unkindly firmness with which the superior five had vindicated their claim to a higher social standing. She leaned through the hedge and said, "Little girl, would you like to come into the wood? It's ever so much nicer than those silly fields."

At the sound of a stranger's voice the little girl jumped back — very like a startled rabbit, the Lady Noggs thought — cast one swift, wary glance behind her to be sure that the coast was clear for flight, then stared at the Lady Noggs with wondering eyes.

"Would you like to come into the wood?" said the Lady Noggs again.

The child shook her head and said: "Mrs. Heldridge said as we weren't to go into no wood — none of us. The keeper would cop us," she said.

"Oh, that's all right," said the Lady Noggs. "This is my uncle's wood, and I can have any one in it I like. Come along. There's a gap in the hedge lower down."

The little girl hesitated, but with a brightening face; then she nodded, and they walked down on either side of the hedge till they reached the gap. The Lady Noggs helped her through it. She stared at the Lady Noggs; then she looked round the wood.

"It's better than the fields, isn't it?" said the Lady Noggs with the air of a proprietor.

The little girl nodded.

"What's your name?" said the Lady Noggs.

"Sue — Sue Gye," said the little girl.

"I shall call you Sue. What would you like to do?" said the Lady Noggs.

"I dunno," said Sue, looking round doubtfully.

"Would you like to go and look for rabbits and squirrels? They always play funnily; and you aon't see them in London," said the Lady Noggs.

"Yus," said Sue. "Honly I mustn't git too fur awye from the village. Mrs. Heldridge told me there was dumplings for dinner, with treacle." She dwelt on the words with the hushed awe of a gourmet describing a triumph of cooking.

"All right," said the Lady Noggs. "We can see plenty of rabbits and squirrels without going far at all. Come along quietly."

Sue came along quietly, and she was shown rabbits and squirrels at play; and she gathered flowers. Indeed, she was soon looking quite dazed by the thronging marvels of this strange world into which she had strayed. As she gathered her flowers, the Lady Noggs plied her with questions, and learned that she came from Druggers' Rents, Poplar; that her father followed the profession of docker; that she had two brothers and three sisters, all older than herself; that she had been sent to the country through the instrumentality of a man called the curick. Indeed, she seemed to have as many marvels to tell the Lady Noggs as the Lady Noggs had to show her; but they were of a less agreeable kind. The Lady Noggs was loth indeed to let her go in time to reach the village for the noon dinner; and before they parted they made an appointment to meet at six that evening at the entrance to the wood on the road between Stonorill village and the castle.

After she had gone, the Lady Noggs went straight back to the castle. She found that, purely as a matter of form, for she had learned long ago the hopelessness of the effort, Miss Caldecott was out looking for her; and when soon afterwards she returned, she scolded her severely for her truancy. The Lady Noggs took the scolding meekly, merely observing, in extenuation of her crime, that the day was so fine she could not help it.

Instead of going for a ride in the afternoon, she did the morning's lessons, and came from them to tea on the lawn. At that meal she seemed thoughtful, so that several times Mr. Borrodaile asked her if anything were weighing on her mind.

She only said, with quiet dignity, "I was thinking."

After tea she went up to the nursery, and, finding her well-meaning but malleable nurse, Mrs. Greenwood there, she said: "I want two of my old frocks. I think they'd better be brown holland ones. And I want a pair of shoes; I suppose they'd better be a pair that are getting old. And I want those stockings which I do not wear, because Miss Caldecott does not like the colour. Please make them into a parcel."

Mrs. Greenwood surveyed her charge with the worried look which nearly always followed any request from her, and said weakly, "What does your ladyship want them for ?"

The Lady Noggs did not deign to answer the question. She had long ago learned that a judicious silence was worth all the explanations in the world. She said quietly, " Please make them into a parcel."

Mrs. Greenwood obeyed fussily, grumbling in an undertone. Her proper course, since she was doubtful about the matter, was to consult Miss Caldecott, but she was far too jealous of her to do anything so reasonable, — a fact of which the Lady Noggs was well aware, and of which she made due use. She collected the garments and packed the parcel under the careless supervision of her young mistress. The Lady Noggs took one of her straw hats from its peg, picked up the parcel, and strolled to the window. A quick glance showed her that the coast was clear, since Miss Caldecott was still on the lawn with Mr. Borrodaile, the Prime Minister, and the three or four guests staying in the house. She walked quickly downstairs out into the shrubberies, and struck across the park to the far corner where the high road runs into the wood. She slipped over a set of posts and rails in the fence, and went down the road. She found Sue sitting on the gate which opens into the wide drive of the wood, and, after greeting her, she said, "I've got something for you. Come along into the wood."

They went down the long grassy drive some fifty yards, then turned into the bushes and came to a little clearing.

"I've got some clothes for you," said the Lady Noggs. And she began to unpack the parcel.

Sue's eyes opened wider and wider as the treasures came into view.

The Lady Noggs spread them out and said, "You'd better change here, and stick your old frock and boots among the bushes."

Sue stared at her with unbelieving eyes. "Are they for me?" she said.

"Yes," said the Lady Noggs. "Of course they're for you."

"Strite?" said Sue.

The Lady Noggs understood that it was a

question, though she did not recognize the form. "Yes, they are, really," she said. "You change."

"Blimy!" said Sue, and she set about the operation with a bewildered air, dazed by this sudden possession of wealth beyond the dreams of ostentation. She fingered each article with awed respect; turned it this way and that, with trembling hands; then stripped off her old clothes with feverish haste. The frock fitted her very well, though, since her body was mostly skin and bone, it was a little large. The stockings were also a little large, but the shoes were an excellent fit. When she had put on the hat she looked quite another creature; it is not too much to say that she had risen fifteen ranks in the social hierarchy.

The Lady Noggs surveyed her carefully; then she said, with some hesitation, "I — I'm afraid you will have to get your hands cleaner to go with those clothes. My hands get dirty, of course, when I've been playing, but they don't get so black as yours."

Sue looked at her grimy hands and said firmly, "S'welp me, I will."

"That's all right," said the Lady Noggs, with some relief at finding her suggestion so readily received.

They packed up the rest of the garments in the paper. Sue stuffed her old frock and boots and hat under a bush; and then they began to talk, or rather the Lady Noggs began again her intimate and searching questions into the matter of Druggers' Rents and the life of the inhabitants of Poplar.

As they talked, the pride of wealth now and again got the better of Sue's manners. A blank silence would follow a question from the Lady Noggs, and she would find her protegé absorbed in the ecstatic contemplation of a boot, or a stocking, or a portion of her frock. Once she took off her hat and regarded it with an admiration very near reverence.

The Lady Noggs bore with this diversion of her beneficiary's attention, and maintained the persistent flow of her questions, for her curiosity grew and grew. When the time came to bid one another good-night, she had acquired an extensive and exceedingly unpleasant knowledge of life in the thriving suburb of Poplar. The sun was low when they parted, and, after arranging to meet at the same trysting-place on the following afternoon, the Lady Noggs said: "If Mrs. Eldridge or any one else asks you where you got those clothes from, tell her that Lady Felicia Grandison gave them to you."

Sue's eyes opened wide, and she said: "Is thet you? Lydy Felishyer Grendison? Blimy! That's a little bit of orl raight for a naimé."

The Lady Noggs walked home with a knitted brow, puzzling over the strange and horrible vista of life Sue had opened before her. She would have liked to believe that Sue was telling her stories, or at least exaggerating; but the matter-of-fact way in which she had set forth her distressing details as matters of no account deprived her of this comfortable thought. However, when she reached home she did not ask any questions about the story she had been told, nor indeed did she mention the fact that she had found a new acquaintance. She had a suspicion that, for one of the absurd reasons which direct the conduct of grown people, this new and interesting intimacy might be closed.

They met the next afternoon at the entrance to the wood. Sue, after greeting her, held out her hands and said, with honest but perhaps excessive pride, "I've scrubbed and scrubbed 'em. They're gittin' cleaner."

It may have been so; but to the eye there was

no appreciable decrease in their blackness. However, time would doubtless tell.

They went into the wood, for the Lady Noggs was resolved not to take any risk of interruption of their intimacy. They talked for a while, always about Druggers' Rents, Poplar; and then they played. Sue was a far more intelligent playmate than the Lady Noggs had found the Princess Wilhelmina of Meiningen-Schwerin, though sometimes her English was quite unintelligible. But as a playmate she had the drawback of meticulousness in the matter of her clothes. She would do nothing which exposed them to the dangers of being dirtied or torn, and the Lady Noggs found it somewhat hampering.

The third day, Friday, was their last day together, since Sue's five-shillings' worth of a cleanly life in the country air ended on the Saturday. She was leaving for Poplar at noon on that day. On the Friday night they said goodbye with no little sadness. But as she was walking home a happy idea came to the Lady Noggs; and she at once began to consider how she could compass it "all herself."

The next morning she came to breakfast in her riding habit, and the Prime Minister, supposing that she had been for a ride before break-

fast and not found time to change, did not ask
her why she was wearing it. As soon as breakfast was over, she hurried off to Mr. Borrodaile,
and, having found him in the library, said:
"Could I have my pocket-money now, Billy,
instead of after lunch? I want it for something
very particular."

She made the request with the important air
of one whose mind is fixed upon great financial
transactions; and Mr. Borrodaile paid over the
five shillings with a readiness which showed a
proper appreciation of this commercial attitude.
She thanked him, and hurried out into the stable-
yard, where Villikins awaited her ready-saddled.
She galloped him over the turf of the park and
trotted quickly down the road to the village.
She stopped before the cottage of Mrs. Eldridge; and at the sight of her distinguished
visitor the old woman hurried out to her, followed by Sue.

The Lady Noggs bade them good-morning
and said, "I want Sue to stop another week,
Mrs. Eldridge. I've brought the five shillings;"
and she held it out.

Bobbing and curtseying, Mrs. Eldridge took
the money and said: "Thank you, your ladyship. It's a good heart you've got, the same as I

told Sue when she come home in them clothes you give her. You thank her little ladyship proper."

But Sue's gratitude was, for the moment, swamped by her joy. Her eyes were shining, and she could only murmur to herself in a hushed voice: "Blimy! Hanother week of hit! Hanother week!"

The Lady Noggs smiled at her and said, "This afternoon?"

She nodded with a look of perfect understanding, and the Lady Noggs rode back to the castle.

That afternoon they met and played in the wood as usual; but the Lady Noggs went away early, for there were several guests staying the week-end with her uncle, and she had been instructed to take her tea with them. It had been put to her as a privilege not usually accorded to persons of her age; but she had received it with a certain amount of scorn, merely saying, with the least enthusiastic possible dryness, "All right; if you want me to, I'll come."

She came, and, since there were four strangers among her uncle's guests, she behaved with admirable dignity. But, unfortunately, she had hardly established her reputation for extreme refinement when the Prime Minister said, somewhat fretfully: "I found the door of the pheasant house open just now. You are so forgetful, Felicia, I suppose you left it open."

"S'welp me, I never did!" said the Lady Noggs.

The four strangers straightened themselves in their chairs with a simultaneous gasp, and stared at her in amazed horror.

"Dear, dear!" said the Prime Minister. "This is very tiresome! Wherever did you pick up that dreadful expression?"

"Is it dreadful?" said the Lady Noggs, blushing a little under the earnest gaze of so many eyes. "They — they say it in Poplar."

CHAPTER NINE

AN UNHAPPY CONFERENCE

MISS CALDECOTT, Mr. Borrodaile, and the Prime Minister, directly they had her to themselves, displayed an equally lively curiosity as to the manner in which the Lady Noggs had acquired her knowledge of the idioms of Poplar. That curiosity, however, met with no encouragement from her. She was gratifying no such idle desires, for she had no intention in the world of being deprived of the interesting and profitable companionship of Sue. At the same time she had not forgotten the horror and surprise of her uncle's guests when that happy phrase "S'welp me, I never did," fell from her lips. At her next meeting with Sue, therefore, she touched lightly on the matter of the Poplar dialect. Sue gave her occasion to introduce the subject by prefacing a mere casual remark with the emphatic word "blimy!"

"I don't think we ought to use the word

'blimy' or 's'welp me,'" said the Lady Noggs in a somewhat apologetic tone. "They told me on Saturday that those words weren't quite nice."

"S'welp me, I won't if you don't like," said Sue, with ready acquiescence.

"Well, then, I don't think we will," said the Lady Noggs, "because, if Miss Caldecott says anything isn't quite nice, you may be sure it isn't."

Accordingly, during that day and the days which followed, the Lady Noggs set herself sedulously to weed out the flowers of Poplar diction from Sue's speech. They cropped up with all the persistence of hardy weeds, but the Lady Noggs did not flag in her efforts; nor did she lose hope, since she reminded herself frequently that Sue's hands had, by scrubbing, been reduced from black to dull grey, and after this great achievement there could be no reason why her speech in its turn should not be cleared of blemishes.

The great obstacle in the way of this clearance seemed to be emotion. Along the general level of conversation Sue would go for a long while without a single " blimy " or " s'welp me "; but the moment the conversation rose above that level, and she grew really excited or angry or joyful, her speech was bejewelled with them. This uncertainty, whether they might not be pouring from her lips in a moment, added greatly, at any rate for the Lady Noggs, to the charm of her talk.

Though her main effort was directed to clearing away the idioms of Poplar, the Lady Noggs also contrived to pursue her enquiries into the lives of the inhabitants of that thriving suburb; and the knowledge she gathered made her go about the world very thoughtful. Her meditative attitude did not escape the watchful eyes of either Miss Caldecott or Mr. Borrodaile; and, since thoughtfulness in the Lady Noggs was a sure precursor of trouble, they observed it with no little disquiet. Several times they compared forebodings. It was on him that the first blow fell.

The Lady Noggs chanced on him in the garden one afternoon as he sat in an easy-chair smoking a cigar after lunch. She stopped before him and said, with a very serious air, "I've been talking to Sue."

"Who is Sue?" said Mr. Borrodaile warily.

"She's one of those little girls from London staying in the village."

"Does she belong to Poplar?" said Mr. Borrodaile with a sudden air of enlightenment.

The Lady Noggs ignored the question, and said gravely: "She's been telling me dreadful things — about poor children. She says they're always being knocked about, and always hungry. And they haven't any warm clothes in winter; and they're cold even in bed because they haven't blankets, only sacks. Now, you're a politician, Billy — "

"I'm not! I'm nothing of the kind!" cried Mr. Borrodaile in hasty defence. "I live among politicians, and my work is political, but I'm not a Member of Parliament, so it's no good your trying to saddle *me* with responsibility!"

The eyes of the Lady Noggs became exceedingly piercing, and she said, "I believe you're frightened."

"I am, and I'm going to stay frightened till I know exactly what you're driving at," said Mr. Borrodaile firmly.

"If I was a man I wouldn't be frightened," said the Lady Noggs with ineffable contempt. "But if you're not a politician yourself, you can make them do things all the same. You can make uncle. Will you make them see after these poor children? I tell you some of them that get knocked about and starved are quite babies."

"No, I'm afraid I can't make them," said Mr.

Borrodaile slowly. "At present they have their hands full with protecting people, — bishops, publicans, speculators, to say nothing of manufactures and industries. Hundreds of people and hundreds of things.

"But the children ought to come first!" said the Lady Noggs. "Grown-ups can look after themselves, can't they ? Nobody beats grown-ups. Nobody beats bishops, or starves them, do they ?"

"Well, no, not exactly," said Mr. Borrodaile, in some discomfort.

"Then what do they want protecting for ?" said the Lady Noggs.

Once more Mr. Borrodaile realized that, in dealing with the Lady Noggs, it was safest to make a clean breast of it, and he said: "Well, the fact is, these people are what is called represented in Parliament. Bishops belong to the House of Lords, and publicans send members to both houses. The poor children do not send members to either house; so there is no one whose business it is exactly to speak for them; and so it is hard to do things for them."

"It's a beastly shame!" said the Lady Noggs.

"But, all the same, there are laws to prevent their being ill-treated; and what's more, there is a Society for the Prevention of Cruelty to Children, just as there is a Society for the Prevention of Cruelty to Animals," said Mr. Borrodaile.

"Sue never heard of them," said the Lady Noggs, shaking her head. "Besides, laws don't feed people, do they?"

Mr. Borrodaile fidgeted in his chair, and then shifted his ground, saying: "Another thing, too, your facts are probably all wrong. This little girl Sue has told you of exceptional cases. She exaggerates."

"Exceptional cases?" said the Lady Noggs, puzzled.

"I mean that only very few children are treated like that," said Mr. Borrodaile; and he felt his manner growing more and more deprecatory.

"But Sue knows of lots!" cried the Lady Noggs.

"Probably she's not very intelligent, and she thinks there are more ill-treated than there really are."

The Lady Noggs considered this new point of view carefully for a little while; then she said: "I think I shall have to go and see for myself. Anyhow, I see you're no good, Billy." And she left him with every appearance of utter scorn.

In his discontent with himself for having assumed a political attitude in the face of her generous sentiments, Mr. Borrodaile missed her most important statement that she would have to go and see for herself.

Mr. Borrodaile having thus failed her, the Lady Noggs cast about for some one else to fill his place of helper of the children of the poor. But, mindful of his aspersions on the statements of Sue, when she went to meet her that afternoon she took with her a pencil and paper. They spent a somewhat painful hour getting down a list of the names of the ill-treated children of Sue's acquaintance, and a few facts of their ill-treatment. It was an interesting product of the human intelligence when it was finished; but if the spelling was bad the facts were worse. The Lady Noggs, with Mr. Borrodaile's suggestion of exaggeration still in her mind, cross-questioned Sue again and again about them. She did not shake one of them. Having this documentary evidence, she made up her mind that her uncle should take Mr. Borrodaile's place as defender of the children of the poor. But before she could assail him, she got wind of the fact that on the following afternoon there was to be a conference at Stonorill between her uncle, the Secretary for War, and the Home Secretary. On the instant she saw how much more advantageous it would be to assail three ministers rather than one. By the next afternoon, therefore, she had thought out her plan of action; and with a view to the most effective appearance, she insisted on putting on one of her most picturesque frocks immediately after lunch, whereas in the ordinary course of things she would have put it on, if she had been caught in time, before tea, when she would meet the ministers. Thus prepared for action she watched from the top of the great staircase their arrival, and saw them ushered into the library, where the Prime Minister and Mr. Borrodaile awaited them. She did not, however, go to them at once, but restrained her impatience, because she thought it better to allow them to get on with the business which had brought them down to Stonorill before she laid hers before them.

The conference was soon absorbed in close and arduous discussion. It had before it a very serious and difficult question of practical politics, the question whether there should be three pockets or four on the new army tunic. It would not seem to be a question upon which the counsel of the Home Secretary would have been of great value; but he had been invited to give his opinion, since he had been Secretary for War in a previous administration.

They had talked for an hour, and were almost about to approach the actual matter they had met to discuss, when the door opened and the Lady Noggs entered the room. She actually entered it; she did not rush in, or burst in, or tumble in; she entered the room with a sedate dignity befitting the head of the family of Grandison. A simultaneous smile wreathed the faces of the Home Secretary and the Secretary for War at the sight of this charming vision; but the Prime Minister after one short gasp of dismay, said sharply: "We are very busy, Felicia! Go away, at once!"

The Lady Noggs nodded with gracious politeness to the two ministers, both of whom were acquaintances; then she said with gentle firmness, "But, uncle, I've come to talk about ever such an important thing that ought to be seen to at once; and it will only take a minute or two."

"Dear, dear! This is very tiresome! What is it?" said the Prime Minister.

His two colleagues lounged back in their chairs smiling; and an expression of extreme wariness gathered on Mr. Borrodaile's face.

"It's about poor children," said the Lady Noggs.

The Prime Minister's face fell in an extreme

discomfiture; and the smiles of his colleagues faded. They looked at the Lady Noggs with an air of something very like guilty defiance.

"Well, what about poor children?" said the Prime Minister in a tone of the last resignation.

"I've learned — at least Sue's told me — that lots of little children belonging to poor people are always being beaten and knocked about. She's seen little children, down to quite babies, awfully hurt!" said the Lady Noggs with growing vehemence. "And they often don't have enough to eat; and cry for hours because they're so hungry. And they're always cold in winter because their clothes are too thin and ragged. They're cold even in bed, because they haven't any blankets, only sacks. It ought to be stopped at once. And as you didn't know anything about it, I thought I'd better come and tell you, and then you'd stop it."

The three ministers had begun to fidget in their chairs; and when she stopped they looked at one another glumly. Then the Prime Minister said unhappily: "Dear, dear! This is very tiresome! We're very busy! We can't talk about that now!"

"Oh, I don't want to waste your time!" said

the Lady Noggs readily. "I only want you to
promise to stop it at once."

The three ministers looked glummer than
ever. Mr. Borrodaile put his elbow on the table,
and rested his face in his hand that he might be
able to wipe away the more easily the irresistible
smiles.

The Prime Minister looked from one to the
other of his colleagues for help or for inspira-
tion. He looked in vain. Then he said with a
groan: "These things are very much exaggerated."

"Oh, no; they aren't!" cried the Lady Noggs
with the same vehemence. "Sue's not heard
about them from any one. She's seen them all
herself. And here's a list of some of the children,
and what was done to them. And she handed the
list to the Prime Minister. He puzzled over it;
then passed it to the Secretary of War; he looked
over it with a growing air of bewilderment, and
passed it to the Home Secretary. The Home Secretary glanced over it, and said desperately:
"Legislation cannot touch these things."

"Why?" The Lady Noggs was puzzled in her
turn.

The Home Secretary looked round the room
with an hunted air; then he said: "They're —

they're — ah — the result of economic conditions."

The happy phrase, so far above her understanding, took the Lady Noggs aback. She looked yet more puzzled, and said: "But you do make laws. I'm always hearing about your making laws. Why can't you make a law to have poor children properly looked after and fed?"

"More bills!" cried the Prime Minister. "Why, we've more legislation before us now than we shall get through in three years!"

"More taxes!" said the Home Secretary.

"But the children ought to come first," said the Lady Noggs doggedly.

The three ministers looked at one another helplessly. Then suddenly, with a great air of relief the Home Secretary said: "The country is not ripe for any more legislation on this matter at present."

The sound of these balmy and reassuring words spread smiles of relief over the faces of his colleagues, and they said with one voice: "True — very true."

"But the poor children are being knocked about and starved now, every day!" said the Lady Noggs.

The Home Secretary made a bolt to the last

refuge of a politician: "Your facts," he said, "your facts are wrong. They are exaggerated. There are a few of these cases of course, but they are very few."

"Yes, yes; of course!" chimed in the Prime Minister. "There are very few cases of cruelty to children; and offenders are always brought to book."

The Lady Noggs's face fell, and she said: "Then you won't stop it?"

"There's nothing to stop, or, at any rate, very little," said the Home Secretary, with a virtuous air.

"Some one has been exaggerating things to you — enormously," said the Secretary for War.

The Lady Noggs looked at them in bitter disappointment. Then she said: "Well, I shall have to make sure." And with that she left them to their discussion.

She went away very gloomy; she did not honour the ministers with the light of her presence at tea. She was in the wood with Sue, discussing the route to Druggers' Rents, and the financial aspect of a visit to them.

During the next five days Stonorill Castle heard more of the condition of the children of the poor than it had heard during the last five centuries. In season and out of season the Lady Noggs talked of nothing else. She had never before been blessed with such an admirable, righteous grievance; and Nature had lavished on her an eminent fitness to make the most of it. She so harried the unfortunate Prime Minister that at last he began to perceive dimly through a mist of practical politics that the condition of the children of the poor was a matter for the attention of legislators. He perceived far more clearly that, if he wished to enjoy peace in his own house, it would have to be dealt with soon. But always when the Lady Noggs pressed him too hard he fell back on the assertion that her facts were wrong.

These continual aspersions on Sue's narration of her experience strengthened the Lady Noggs in her purpose of going to see for herself. Her discussions in Stonorill Castle on the condition of the children of the poor alternated with discussions with Sue in the wood, discussions of ways and means of going to observe that condition for herself. Before the five days had elapsed she had made her simple plan; and she obtained sinews of action by a rigorous collection of donations to the children of the poor from her uncle's guests.

On the sixth day she did not breakfast with the Prime Minister; and he ate that meal in an unwonted, grateful peace. He was going to his work with an unusually even mind, when the news came that the Lady Noggs, Villikins, and the governess-cart were missing. Had it been only the Lady Noggs and Villikins that were missing, no one should have taken any notice of the matter; but the absence of the governess-cart awoke suspicion.

Miss Caldecott set inquiries afoot; and a groom sent out to gather information came back with the news that the Lady Noggs and a slum child of the name of Gay had been seen driving on the road to Warlesden. Miss Caldecott informed the Prime Minister at once of this news, and he despatched a mounted groom to Warlesden. The groom returned with the information that the Lady Noggs had left Villikins and the governess-cart at the Crown Inn, and left for London by the 7.15 train, with another little girl. He had also learned that she had asked for tickets to Poplar. By a great expenditure of motor car tires, the Prime Minister, Mr. Borrodaile, and Miss Caldecott caught the 10.15.

The Lady Noggs had formed her plan with great judgment. At six o'clock that morning she had harnessed Villikins to the governess-cart, unseen and unheard by the slothful stableman who still slept. She picked up Sue on the further side of Stonorill village, and they reached Warlesden in plenty of time to hand over the pony and trap to the incurious ostler of the Crown Inn, and catch the 7.15 to London. The Lady Noggs took third-class single tickets, for as she justly observed, her relatives would pay their return fares; and she wanted as much money as possible to spend on the poor children when she found them.

CHAPTER TEN

THE PERILS OF PHILANTHROPY

WHEN Sue and the Lady Noggs reached London, they were some little time learning the road to that vague land known to Sue as Out-Poplar-Way. At last having learned it, they went in a cab to Fenchurch Street; and the bluff and hearty cabman, moved by the youth and innocence of his fares, bluffly and heartily took from the Lady Noggs two shillings more than his due.

From Fenchurch Street a slow and steady train carried them with evident reluctance and every possible stoppage to Poplar. In the grime of that thriving suburb Sue was at home, and took the post of leader. Uncomfortable, and full of questions, the Lady Noggs followed her down long mean street after long mean street. She wanted to collect all the hungry, ragged children she met; but Sue promised her hungrier and raggeder children, if she would wait. At last she brought her round the back of a timber-yard into one of those striking and admirable monuments of twentieth-century civilization, a warren of the submerged. It was a row of four eighteenth-century houses of a fair size but dilapidated condition, of paneless, rag-stuffed windows, crooked gables, tottering chimney-stacks, and bulging or sinking roofs full of holes; the very profitable property of a well-known sporting haberdasher whose yacht is the last cry of nautical luxury. A din of harsh, high-pitched voices came from the paneless windows and open doors through the heavy, malodorous air which no breeze seemed to have stirred for weeks; and in the gutter or the deep dust of the roadway, sat or played listlessly in the heat, a score of the children the Lady Noggs had come to see, gaunt, dirty, ragged little savages.

The Lady Noggs and Sue were dressed in plain holland frocks and sailor hats, but at once the children gathered round them crying to one another, half curious, half hostile. Untorn clothes, clean faces, and kempt hair were rarities unlikely to escape notice in Druggers' Rents.

The Lady Noggs looked round at the gaunt little faces, in a horror at a reality so much worse than her imaginations, pulled herself together, and said to a little girl of about her own age, who was carrying a frail scrap of a baby with large eyes in a tiny white face, "Would you like a meal?"

"Garn!" said the little girl distrustfully.

"It's strite," said Sue, in the children's own tongue. "She's not a-gittin' at yer. She's goin' ter treat yer."

A shrill clamour of extreme excitement rose from the children; they pressed forward urging their claims, or fawning on the Lady Noggs with the professional beggar whine.

"But can I feed them all?" said the Lady Noggs.

Sue nodded: "You can pay for more than them," she said.

A big Irish girl strolled lazily up from the nearest doorway, and said, "Fwhat is ut?"

A dozen excited children told her of the Lady Noggs's offer. She lost her laziness and said, "Begorra, but ut's a meal they want!" And with the national aptitude for organization, she took the matter in hand.

She marshalled the children into a column, started them out of the Rents, and brought up the rear with Sue and the Lady Noggs. As they went the Lady Noggs explained to her the purpose of her journey to this lost land; and when the girl understood, she said, "Is ut knocking about and starvation ye want to see?" and called back child after child from the column, saying to one, "Allus, me darlint, show the little lady the bruishze on y'r leg ye got from y'r dad Sathurday noight;" to another, "Tommy, me man, where's them wales ye got from y'r grandmother lasth toime she was in the drink?" to a third, "Jimmy, y'r ribs are asier t' count than most, give the little lady a look at them." The children, who called the girl Norry, did her bidding with alacrity; the clothes of the mites were of no wholeness to prevent the display of their scars; and the Lady Noggs, sickened by the sights, had lost all pleasure in her benevolence long before they had turned into the inconceivably dirty little eating-house which was their goal, and the children were clamouring at the noxious-looking old woman who kept it, for food. The Lady Noggs gave Norry her purse, and she displayed a sovereign from it. By the sight of it the old woman was affected to a briskness beyond her years; and plate after plate was loaded with food and set on the filthy tables to which the knives and forks, black from point to handle, were strongly chained.

The dish of the day was that eighteenth-century delicacy, beef *a-la-mode*, procured to all seeming from the stables of a neighbouring tramway terminus; evil-looking chunks of it flanked by doubtful potatoes and besmeared with a thick mahogany-coloured grease filled the plates. Tears of joy filled the eyes of some of the children at the sight of this good cheer; and all of them fell on it with a savage gusto, their eyes glintening, their mouths watering, silent, absorbed in a luxurious delight.

But when the Lady Noggs saw ravenous little babies getting a share from the plates of those who carried them, she cried out against it: "They must have milk!" she said. "They must have milk!"

At such lavishness a kind of stupefaction fell on some of the little girls: they paused in their eating for as long as ten seconds to stare at her with unbelieving eyes. But Norry rose to the occasion: she said to a lanky, ferret-faced youth, who had been sitting at a table when they came in, "Go to Mother Butterick's, an' bring eighteen-pennorth of the best, an' see it is the best, will yer?"

She spoke as one used to command, and the youth shambled out. He did not come back;

but presently a stout, red-faced woman came to the door with a milk can. Norry sniffed it distrustfully, passed it, and paid her. Then each babe was provided with a dirty cup full of its natural food; and the feast resumed its way.

The children ate and ate; their faces flushed, and their eyes grew drowsy. At last one by one they began to lay down their knives and forks with heavy sighs; and no loud encouragement from Norry could urge them to further efforts. The elders sat still and silent; the babies fell asleep; and the little toddlers had laid their heads on the table and slept, too. Norry paid the bill, and by dint of firmness got them out of the eating-house. They stood in the street, a sleepy band; she extracted three thin, sleepy cheers for the little lady from them, and started them off to their dismal homes. Then she said to the Lady Noggs, "Here's y'r purrse, me darlint; there's twelve bob left in ut; an' God bless y'r pretty face and koind harrt."

The Lady Noggs shook her head, and said, "No: you keep it, and buy them some more food to-morrow. And, oh! Do give the babies milk! I'll send you some more sometimes out of my pocket-money, you know. Where shall I send it to you?"

"Shure, y're a little angel! Sind it to Miss Norry Murphy, Druggers' Rents Poplar. And fwhat's yor name, me little darlint?"

The Lady Noggs hesitated: some curious shame at the contrast between their lots restrained her from giving it: it did not seem a name to be uttered outside that eating-house; she said hastily, "You can call me Noggs. They call me Noggs at home."

"And a blessed name ut is!" said Norry.

"There isn't anything else I can do, is there? Now, I mean," said the Lady Noggs anxiously.

"Sorra wan; but maybe you'll be coming to see us agin?"

"I'll try; but I mayn't be allowed."

"Well, here's yor purrse, me darlint. I'll do as ye wish wiv the twelve bob. Take the fifth torrning on the lift, an' you'll come to the station. I musth be after thim childer, or they'll be slaping in the middle av the road. Goodboye, an' God bless ye!"

She kissed them, and hurried off; they waved their hands to her when she looked over her shoulder, till she passed out of sight. Then they turned, and set out for the station. The Lady Noggs walked in silence for fifty yards; then she

said, "Oh, those poor children! You were quite
right, Sue."

There was a sudden rush from an alley they
were passing; and five Hooligans dashed out
upon them, led by the lanky, ferret-faced youth
who had gone from the eating-house to order the
milk. In a twinkling the Lady Noggs's purse had
been torn from her pocket and the gold bangles
from her wrists; two of the boys had her by the
arms, and were hurrying her down the alley,
two others were dealing in like manner with Sue.
The children were the captives of those romantic but blackguardly products of the Board
School and the Penny Dreadful, the Poplar
Claud Duvals, a band of vicious louts who ter-
rorized the less policed streets of that thriving
suburb.

As they hurried them along, their captors
with horrible threats bade them hold their
tongues; and the Lady Noggs was too dazed
by the suddenness of the events to resist, even
had she been less firmly gripped. The Poplar
Claud Duvals were bragging to one another
ferociously of the swiftness of their deadly
swoop, like boys at play; and she gathered from
their talk that they were going to hold her and
Sue to ransom. She was beginning to understand

Five Hooligans dashed out upon them

that they were in a perilous plight, when they came out of the further end of the alley into a street even meaner than the one they had left, and almost ran into a very large red-bearded, red-headed sailor.

"Sailor! Sailor! Help us! We're being carried a— " shrieked the Lady Noggs; and a blow on the mouth cut her short.

The sailor seemed a man of alertness, for on the instant his heavy stick whacked down on the youth who had struck her, and laid him low; and before the Poplar Claud Duvals realized what was happening, he had another by the throat with his left hand and his stick was playing about the heads of the other three. In less than twenty seconds two of them were yelling with anguish; and the scattered wits of the third were only collected by the teeth of the Lady Noggs, turned to a little wild cat by the blow on her mouth, meeting in the hand which held her. He raised his yell in unison; and the three of them bolted down the street. The sailor banged the head of his captive against the wall with a cheery whooping, and despatched him after his friends with a kick of singular propulsion. Then he turned to the children, and said, "This ain't no neighbourhood for us, kiddies!" tucked his

stick under his arm; caught either by the hand;
and rushed them up the alley.

They came into the street of the eating-house;
hurried down it, up a turning to the left, and
came to a sudden breathless stop before another very large sailor coming down it.

"Hullo, Albert! Starting a family?" said the
other large sailor.

The rescuer made no answer; he wiped his
brow with a handkerchief of intensest brilliance,
and burst into a stentorian bellow of,

> *"In Burdo Town! In Burdo Town!*
> *We laid 'em out! We knocked 'em down!*
> *Frenchies, Da-agos, whi-ite an' brown!*
> *We la-id 'em out in Burdo Town!"*

At the end of this pæan he burst into a huge
Homeric laughter, and told of his battle with
the five Hooligans. Then he turned to the
Lady Noggs, and asked her where her mammy
lived.

"I haven't got one," said the Lady Noggs. "I
want to get to the Duchess of Huddersfield's in
Berkeley Square. I'm Lady Felicia Grandison;
and I came down to this beastly hole to find out
whether poor children are starved and knocked
about! I know all about it now; and I want to

get home!" She spoke fiercely, for she was still raging at the blow.

"So you shall, my lass! So you shall!" said Albert; and he stooped and wiped her bleeding lip with the handkerchief of intensest brilliance. Then he straightened himself, and said, "Jerry, what ho! This is a little ladyship what I've rescooed. We must make an effort, my lad, an' take 'er 'ome befittinglike — in a 'ansom."

"P'raps 'er little ladyship 'ud like a drink — a glass of red port wine," said Jerry rising to the proper height.

"No, thank you," said the Lady Noggs. "I only want to get to my aunt's."

"I wonder at you, Jerry!" said Albert in sad reproach. "Where's your tone? Pubs ain't for the likes of them! Come along your ladyship; an' we'll find a cab."

As they sought one the Lady Noggs related to the sympathetic and charmed mariners the story of her errand to Druggers' Rents, and of her capture. When they at last found a hansom, Albert took the Lady Noggs on his knee, and Jerry took Sue on his. They talked with great friendliness as they drove mile after mile through that dismal quarter towards civilization; but slowly Albert grew more and more silent and absorbed: he seemed to have a weight on his mind. Suddenly, in Fleet Street, he brightened, and said, "This is 'ow it ought to ha' run, Jerry,

> "*In Poplar Town! In Poplar Town!*
> *I laid 'em out! I knocked 'em down!*
> *Fi-ive to one I di-id 'em brown!*
> *I la-id 'em out in Po-oplar Town!*"

He produced this new version of his pæan in the same terrific bellow; and the passing throng paused at the rush of sound to stare open-mouthed at the cab.

"You be a wonner, Albert!" said Jerry with convinced admiration.

And the Lady Noggs said with equal admiration, "You have a splendid voice."

"It ain't every one," said Albert with thoughtful gratification, "as is praised by a lady of title, 'owever young."

He was so proud of this child of his imagination that he sang it again in the Strand, in the Haymarket, in Piccadilly, and Berkeley Square was echoing the strain when the cab stopped before Hartlepool House. They got out; and suddenly the size of the house filled the sailors with a bashful confusion. After an incoherent farewell they were tumbling over one another back into the cab, when the Lady Noggs took command: "Come out!" she said sternly. "You've got to come and see my aunt, and be thanked properly!" And she caught Albert by the arm, disregarded his protest, and pulled him up the steps. Sue and Jerry followed.

"The butler will pay the cab," she said; and rang the bell.

"Tell Wilkins to pay the cab," she said to the astonished footman; and led the reluctant Albert past him; opened the door of the dining-room, and brought him in. Half her family were seated round the table, drinking their coffee after lunch and smoking, while they debated further measures for her recovery, and awaited news from Scotland Yard and the police stations of Poplar.

"How do you do, aunt?" said the Lady Noggs, running to the duchess and kissing her. "This is Albert and Jerry. Albert is awfully brave! He fought five Hooligans except one which I bit, and rescued us, or I don't know what we should have done! They had taken us captives, you know, and were going to keep us! And he has a splendid voice: you should hear him sing! Mr. Albert, Mr. Jerry, the Duchess of Huddersfield."

Her family, though greatly relieved by her unexpected arrival in its midst, was taken aback. It could never grow used, though it enjoyed plentiful opportunities, to her habit of suddenly dumping perfect strangers into its bosom, and it gazed at the gallant mariners with some discomfort, showing a distressing lack of presence of mind at being suddenly confronted with them. For their part, the gallant mariners showed not a whit less discomfort.

The duchess was the first to recover, and she greeted the little party. Then the duke and some of his guests recovered enough to pour a flood of questions on the Lady Noggs. The only result was a general incoherence. Then the butler was summoned, and the duchess bade him take Albert and Jerry to the servants' hall and feast them; and also make haste to send a wire to the Poplar police, informing them of the return of the Lady Noggs, and bidding them inform the Prime Minister, Miss Caldecott, Mr. Borrodaile, and the other searchers who had gone to the far East to hunt for her, and were wandering feverishly about Poplar.

The Lady Noggs said that she and Sue were very hungry. The servants were ordered to bring them lunch; and they ate it to an accompani-

"Mr. Albert, Mr. Jerry, the Duchess of Huddersfield"

ment of scores of questions which drew from
the Lady Noggs a fairly coherent account of
their adventures. When she had gratified their
curiosity she began to dilate at length on the
children of Druggers' Rents. She painted a picture of their scars, hunger, and rags, which
pierced in the most unpleasant fashion the comfort in which her hearers were lapped.

When she had done the duke said with natural heat, "Look here, Noggs; you've no business to go to such places — no business at all!
It must stop! It's not only the Hooligans, but
such places are hot-beds of disease. You might
catch any fever there!"

"I didn't want to go!" cried the Lady Noggs.
"But Billy and uncle, and both those two stupid
politicians said that Sue was wrong — that children weren't really treated like that — and I
had to go and see for myself. And Sue was quite
right, just as I thought. You belong to the
House of Lords; why don't you see after the
poor children?"

The Duke said, "Ah — hum!" and became
discreetly silent.

The Lady Noggs went on to give a description of Albert's pæan, which she plainly regarded
as one of the supreme efforts of modern poetic

genius. There was no one in that exalted assembly capable of criticising her pronouncement.

After they had finished their lunch the two sailors were summoned to the dining-room. They were thanked by the duke, and handsomely rewarded; but the Lady Noggs pressed Albert to sing in vain: he seemed the unresisting prey of an invincible shyness.

CHAPTER ELEVEN

MR. BORRODAILE IS FIRM

THE economy of the Lady Noggs in taking third-class single tickets to London was, as she had anticipated, justified by her uncle taking herself and Sue back to Warlesden first-class. Her expedition to investigate the condition of the children of the poor, distressing as it had been, was satisfactory to her in that it had demonstrated the truth of Sue's assertions. It was in no way satisfactory to anybody else, since it had provided her with excellent grounds for urging her uncle, Mr. Borrodaile, and any politician who came to Stonorill, to do something for those children.

The expedition, however, in one way proved unfortunate for her: it brought to the notice of her elders the existence of Sue as her intimate, and also the kind of intimate she was. At first they were for letting the intimacy continue for the two or three days yet to elapse before Sue's

return to Druggers' Rents; then they learned
that she owed the week she was enjoying in the
country, to the bounty of the Lady Noggs; and
lastly they learned that the Lady Noggs proposed to make the intimacy a perpetual companionship. At once they began to seek a gentle
and decorous method of bringing it to an
end.

One morning the Prime Minister came into
the breakfast-room to find the Lady Noggs
already there. The sight disquieted him, for he
had never known her punctual save with a view
to compassing some unadvisable end. Conse-
quently during the early part of the meal he
was on his guard and maintained a watchful
attitude which he found somewhat tiring. It
seemed that his suspicions were unfounded.
She did not attack him on the burning question
of the condition of the children of the poor; she
talked on indifferent subjects, of the European
situation, and of the relatives she had met at
her aunt's on her expedition to London. Her
mind seemed so free from any serious matter
that he was lulled into a security for which he
had no justification.

Suddenly, when he was least expecting it, the
attack opened, and the Lady Noggs said, "Un-

cle, I don't want Sue to go back to Druggers' Rents."

"Sue?" said the Prime Minister. "Ah, yes; the little girl who took you to that slum the other day."

"Yes; I want her to come and live with me."

"To come and live with you?"

"Yes; you've often said that I ought to have a companion as old as myself."

"But she's not at all the kind of little girl to be your companion."

"Why; what's the matter with her? She's very nice," said the Lady Noggs. And her air was resolute indeed.

The Prime Minister looked round somewhat helplessly; then he said, "She — she doesn't speak nicely — and the kind of life she's led — oh, it wouldn't do at all!"

"She speaks just as well as the Princess Wilhelmina — only different," said the Lady Noggs.

"Her manners — " the Prime Minister began.

"They're just as good as the Princess Wilhelmina's," said the Lady Noggs cutting him short. "She eats quite as nicely — nicelier."

The Prime Minister driven into a corner turned to bay: "Dear, dear! This is very tiresome!" he said. "I'm not going to discuss the matter. She cannot come to live with you."

The Lady Noggs saw quite plainly that on this occasion she had failed to bend her uncle to her purpose; but that by no means caused her to abandon her attempt to get her way. She made up her mind to try again later. In the meantime, just to go on with as it were, she fell to a disappointed grumbling. She alleged that when he wanted her to go to that horrid Catford he had said that it would be good for her to have a little girl to play with always; and now that she'd found a little girl he wouldn't let her have one.

The Prime Minister was unhappy since there was just enough of a suspicion of justice in her complaint to worry his scrupulous soul.

However, he kept silence with a wisdom very rare in him, and at last his niece said, "Well, anyhow; I don't want her to go and be knocked about and starved in Druggers' Rents, just because there's nobody to look after poor little children. Could I have her for my maid?"

The Prime Minister could never miss a chance of a compromise. Compromise always brought balm to his scrupulous soul; it was probably dearer to it than German philosophy. He said with real warmth, "Now that is a much more feasible idea. It used to be the custom in English families to take servants into the house as children and let them grow up in it. My grandmother did it, and even my mother."

"Then I may?" said the Lady Noggs, surprised at his readiness.

"Well, well — not at once — not at once," said the Prime Minister. "We shall have to find some institution or school where she can be taught to speak properly first; then we can try it."

"All right," said the Lady Noggs, with no show of gratitude. "I suppose I must make that do."

But though she was but little satisfied with this concession, Sue was overjoyed; and in the fulness of her emotion reverted to the idioms, racy of the slum, which obtain Out-Poplar-Way. She said with a certain shrillness, "S'welp me! But that's a little bit of horl ryght!"

It chanced that Miss Caldecott was reading that evening in the rose garden, when she became aware that Mr. Borrodaile was coming down the path; and when he sat down in the garden chair in front of her, she perceived his uncommonly resolute air with no little disquiet.

She found that his eyes were for the while too masterful for her own to meet; and while she preserved an appearance of unruffled, innocent carelessness, her spirit girded on its womanly armour to meet the crisis.

"Violet," said Mr. Borrodaile quietly.

"Miss Caldecott!" she interrupted quickly.

"Violet," Mr. Borrodaile repeated firmly, "I am going to talk seriously for a change."

"Please don't," said Miss Caldecott.

"Why not?"

"It's no use."

"That remains to be seen," said Mr. Borrodaile; and bending suddenly forward he caught her pretty hands in a firm grasp, and paying no heed to her efforts to draw them away, said, "Will you marry me?"

Miss Caldecott blushed and her eyes shone. "Of course not!" she cried.

"Why not?" said Mr. Borrodaile.

"Why — why — the idea is absurd, you know it is."

"No, I don't. Why is it absurd?"

"Of course it is!" cried Miss Caldecott; and she grew somewhat confused. "There is your career — you must marry in accordance with it — somebody rich — everybody says so. Politics are growing more and more a matter of money every day; and you must. Besides, it is all settled, you know it is."

"Settled?" said Mr. Borrodaile in some surprise. "Oh, do you mean Miss Morgan?"

"Yes," said Miss Caldecott, and she tugged harder at her fettered hands.

"Well" — said Mr. Borrodaile coolly without loosening them — "so far other people have done all the settling. For my part, I have decided never to ask Miss Morgan to marry me unless she chances to be the only woman left in the world, so that you are quite right in saying that that's settled."

"It doesn't matter. You've got to marry a rich wife; and you've no business to talk to me like this. Why — why it would spoil your career — absolutely!"

"We'll put my career aside," said Mr. Borrodaile indulgently. "It hasn't got anything to do with the matter."

"Oh, yes, it has! Everything!" Miss Caldecott protested.

"Nothing at all," said Mr. Borrodaile. "There is only one thing that has anything to do with it and that is — Do you care for me enough to marry me?"

Miss Caldecott gasped; then looking almost as determined as Mr. Borrodaile, she said in a low but quite firm voice, "No: I don't."

"And I thought you so truthful," said Mr. Borrodaile sadly.

Miss Caldecott's face became of a singularly vivid scarlet: "How dare you?" she cried. "I don't! I don't! I don't!"

"Can you look me in the face and say that?" said Mr. Borrodaile.

Miss Caldecott looked him in the face full and square, and said with heated firmness, "I don't!"

Mr. Borrodaile let go her hands and rose: "Ah, well," he said sorrowfully, "there's nothing more to be said." And he turned and walked slowly out of the rose garden.

Miss Caldecott watched him go. At first her eyes were angry, then they softened; she opened her mouth to call him back, and shut it quickly at the bidding of duty. When he had gone through the gate, she sank back in her chair trembling; but her conscience warmly applauded her action, and she could not see the rose-bush in front of her for the rising tears. Then she began to cry softly: it was one thing to be applauded by her conscience, but quite another to endure the clamouring reproaches of her heart at the renunciation.

Mr. Borrodaile had walked out of the main gate of the rose garden with a singularly dejected air. But once out of sight of Miss Caldecott, he straightened his back, turned to the right, and with noiseless footsteps went up the path along the rose garden wall and re-entered it by a side door. Keeping on the grass border of the path in his noiseless, rubber-soled tennis shoes he came quietly to a point where he could get a view of the cruel fair, and saw her leaning forward with her face in her hands. There came into his eyes a light of triumph; he stole right up to her, dropped quietly on one knee, and slipping an arm round her, said gently, "Never mind, Violet. I knew you didn't mean it." And as she drew her hands sharply away from her face, he kissed her.

"Oh!" she cried; and her face flamed. "How dare you? Oh, what a mean thing to do! Spying — absolutely spying!"

The ferocity of her tone was belied by the thankfulness in her eyes; and Mr. Borrodaile took advantage of her extreme indignation to kiss her again.

She sprang out of the chair with a vigour that

upset him, and faced him panting and with flashing eyes, apparently at a loss for the right word, for twice or thrice she opened her mouth to speak and shut it again.

Mr. Borrodaile sat where he had been shoved, to all seeming, in perfect content, and met her infuriated gaze with steady, not to say, brazen eyes: "At any rate, that settles it," he said.

Miss Caldecott stamped her foot and cried in a tone in which the anger and appeal were about evenly blended, "It doesn't!"

Mr. Borrodaile rose with great deliberation and said, "Oh, yes; it does. You must see that the situation is entirely changed."

"It is not!" cried Miss Caldecott.

"Well," said Mr. Borrodaile with something of judicial impartiality in his tone and air, "if you can give me an explanation of the fact that you were crying which does not change the situation, I'll admit I'm wrong."

She was taken aback for the moment; then, swiftly shifting her ground, she cried, "I think you're detestable! Spying like that!"

"Spying? Spying?" said Mr. Borrodaile almost plaintively. "Why I only came back to ask if there was any chance of your changing your mind, and found you had already changed it."

"Oh!" cried Miss Caldecott. "What is one to say to you?" And truly she looked at a loss.

"Well there are lots of nice things you might say, things I have been wanting to hear you say for ever so long, ever since I first saw you. You might say, "William, I will marry you as soon as it can be arranged."

"But I won't!" said Miss Caldecott firmly.

"Well, I don't mind your not saying it as long as you do it," said Mr. Borrodaile with a fine show of generosity.

"But I won't do it! I will not!"

"Oh, yes; you will now — now that you've been crying," said Mr. Borrodaile. "Let us sit down and discuss the matter quietly."

Miss Caldecott with unimpaired vigour refused to do anything of the kind, and Mr. Borrodaile strolled back with her to the house, discussing the matter quietly as he went. She did not take any part in the discussion, but she carried her head very high. On the threshold she turned and said, "I shall not."

Mr. Borrodaile did not say anything; he had said all he wanted to say for the time being.

For the next two or three days Miss Caldecott treated him with extreme coldness, and kept him at the furthest possible distance. He seemed quite contented with this treatment, for he was willing to give her reasonable time to grow used to the situation in which her fortunate tears had placed her. But he wished that he had been firmer with the scruples which had led him to inform the Prime Minister that he was going to ask his niece's governess to marry him; for the ladies of his family, headed by the Duchess of Huddersfield, descended on Stonorill to protest against the spoiling of his political future. He was not indeed, surprised that the Prime Minister had informed them of the matter, for he knew his readiness to avoid any responsibility which his scrupulous conscience did not force upon him; but he was taken aback by the suddenness of the descent.

The ladies did not immediately assail him. First they held conferences among themselves on the matter. These conferences strengthened the strong conviction they already entertained of the impossibility of the marriage. The duchess, whose kindliness of heart is only equalled by her knowledge of the world, summed up the feeling of the members of the conferences when she said, "It will not do. Violet is a dear girl and the daughter of one of my oldest friends;

we ought never to have let her take up this
absurd governessing; we ought to have taken
her and married her to some one nice — a — a
banker or an attorney-general, some one pleasant who could have given her the right position.
But of course she wouldn't let us. These new
stupid ideas of independence — if a girl gets
hold of them, there's no doing anything with
her, unless you shut her up and feed her on
bread and water, as Lady Blyde treated Agnes
Blyde, till she's cured. Of course we couldn't do
that with Violet, for she's an orphan and there's
no one who has the right to do it for her. And it
did seem an excellent arrangement that she
should look after Felicia and teach her; and
now the result is that unless we are very careful
and firm, William's career will be spoiled. Of
course Beresford Caldecott ought to make her
an allowance; he's her uncle and neither of them
have any other near relations in the world; certainly he ought to. A couple of thousand a year
would be nothing to him. But there, it is no
good talking of that. Beresford Caldecott is just
the most impossible person in the world. I
should have thought a man who had had his
early training, though he had the worst temper
I ever came across and ran away from home,

might have made a million in South America without growing into such a terribly offensive person. But it seems he couldn't; and so we cannot look for any help from him."

The upshot of the conferences was that the duchess was deputed to discuss the matter with Miss Caldecott and offer her nicely, though of course not in so many words, a banker or attorney-general; and she was further deputed to reason with Mr. Borrodaile. She set about these matters at once, and was very pleased to find that Miss Caldecott shared the feelings of the rescuers and was no less resolved than they that Mr. Borrodaile's career must not be sacrificed to a romantic but unsuitable marriage founded on reasons of sentiment rather than sense. But Mr. Borrodaile, whom the duchess left to the last, knowing of old that he was an extremely difficult person to manage, proved himself quite intractable. He showed a painful but steady disinclination to admit that the rational point of view was of chief importance in the matter, an attitude very difficult to deal with by reason of its inherent absurdity; and he was the more disposed to give the kind ladies trouble because their supporting presence added greatly to the resisting power of Miss Caldecott.

At this stage Miss Caldecott's engaging pupil somehow or other became aware of what was in the wind. Members of the rescuing band were apt to discuss the situation out of season, and with little heed to whether they were alone or not. One morning after breakfast therefore the Lady Noggs came upon Mr. Borrodaile, and broke into his gloomy meditations with the sage observation, "I think marrying's silly."

At the moment it was the last sentiment with which Mr. Borrodaile was in sympathy; he had heard from so many people during the last few days that marrying, or rather a particular marriage, was silly. And only the night before Miss Caldecott had shown herself more resolute than ever to be no party to the absurdity. He looked at the Lady Noggs with unkindly eyes, and said nothing.

"I think marrying's silly," said the Lady Noggs again.

"That's it, be feminine, hit a man when he's down. The peerage has no sense of fair play," said Mr. Borrodaile.

"I am not feminine! And it has!" said the Lady Noggs quickly and with heat, showing her usual touchiness in the matter of the peerage, "Besides, you're not down, are you?"

"Do I look up?" said Mr. Borrodaile gloomily.

"You don't look happy," said the Lady Noggs, regarding him with closer attention. "Can I do anything for you?"

Mr. Borrodaile shook his head: "I'm afraid you can't," he said. "But all the same, thanks very much for the offer. You're the only person who has offered to help me. All the rest have been active volunteers in the work of putting spokes in my wheel."

"Perhaps I can do something," said the Lady Noggs, with an air of serious good will.

"I don't think anybody can except Beresford Caldecott, and he is hardly the man to do it," said Mr. Borrodaile thoughtfully.

"I might try," said the Lady Noggs hopefully.

"I'm afraid it's no good," said Mr. Borrodaile. "These delicate matters don't afford much scope for a helper." And he rose to go to the Prime Minister.

The Lady Noggs walked with him into the house, left him at the door of the Prime Minister's study, and went on herself to the schoolroom.

CHAPTER TWELVE

THE IMPOSSIBLE UNCLE

MISS CALDECOTT found her uncommonly absent-minded at her lessons that morning, as was indeed natural, seeing that her mind was rather busied with a problem of sentimentality rather than with the sprightly elusiveness of the French irregular verbs. She had acquired a very fair knowledge of the reasons of her governess's obduracy, but she did not know how Beresford Caldecott came into the matter. She was not one, however, to allow a lack of directness to stand in the way of a good end, and when lessons were over and the tiresome books had been put away, she turned to Miss Caldecott and said, "Who's Beresford Caldecott?"

"He's my uncle," said Miss Caldecott. "Why?"

"What sort of an uncle is he?" said the Lady Noggs.

Miss Caldecott shrugged her shoulders and said, "Why do you want to know?"

"Ah! I thought he wasn't a nice uncle," said the Lady Noggs.

"What do you mean?" said Miss Caldecott.

"When you ask people about any one who's nice they say so straight away," said the Lady Noggs. "And when he isn't nice, they don't tell you anything."

"I see," said Miss Caldecott. "But why did you want to know?"

The Lady Noggs shook her head. "That's a secret," she said. And Miss Caldecott forebore to press her.

The relations of Mr. Borrodaile and Miss Caldecott were beginning to move in quite the wrong direction, and both of them were on the way to resentment. Mr. Borrodaile was beginning to take her avoidance of him hard; and she was beginning to grow vexed at his obdurate refusal to accept her decision. Matters were very much at a deadlock, and Mr. Borrodaile was beginning to think that he had better go away on a holiday, or if he did not take a holiday, at any rate, remove himself to town and do his work there. Then one evening he had dressed,

and was in the great hall waiting for the dinner
gong, when the Lady Noggs descended on him,
and said with the most businesslike directness,
"How can Berresford Caldecott help?"

Mr. Borrodaile looked at her gloomily and
was about to evade the question, when he remembered that the Lady Noggs would probably worry him somewhat till she got an answer. "Well, since you insist on knowing," he
said, "the idea is, that he should make Violet
an allowance."

"And won't he?" said the Lady Noggs.

"He has never been approached on the subject; but there's a general impression among
those who have had the pleasure of a slight acquaintance with him, that wild horses would not
drag an allowance from him."

"But if nobody's asked, how do they know?"
said the Lady Noggs.

"You have hit on the weak point in their position," said Mr. Borrodaile.

"I think they're silly not to have asked him,"
said the Lady Noggs. "Good-night."

As she went up-stairs, she was making up her
mind that Mr. Beresford Caldecott must be
approached, at once, and by letter. But she
sighed as she came into the nursery at the

thought of the difficult task before her: the writing of such an important letter was not a mere matter of a few easy minutes with a pencil; it meant a painful struggle with pen and ink. She was, indeed, tempted to write in pencil; but she decided that the letter would lose weight, if transacted in such a medium; and she braced herself to the harder effort.

She set the ink, now confined to its little pot, but soon to be spreading all about the room and its occupants, on the table, and hunted out a pen and blotting pad. From it she tore the top sheet, and set it ready to cover the letter should Miss Caldecott enter, discover its purport, and forbid her writing it. Then she sat down and squared her elbows to the task.

Its difficulties began early. It was no easy matter to decide whether to write "Dear Sir" or "Dear Mr. Caldecott." But by dint of nibbling firmly the end of her pen she found the solution: she could write the letter in the third person. Accordingly she set about it, and at the end of a half an hour's patient struggle, she had finished the rough draft. Then with a splendid endurance she copied it. When it was done there was much more ink on the Lady Noggs than on the paper. It ran: —

Lady Felicia Grandison pressents her complements to Mr. Burysford Caldicott and wishes to ask him if you will give Violet an allowance: then she could marry Mr. Borrodaile and everyboddy would be satisfyd. I think you really ought and then she would not look so miserrable no more would Billy.

She looked at the engaging exposition of the facts of the case with no little pride. There was only one blot worth speaking of on it; and none of the smudges really impaired its legibility for any one gifted with unusually keen eyes. She put it in an envelope, and on it she wrote Mr. Burysford Caldicott. Then she remembered that she didn't know where that gentleman lived. She thought, however, that she would have no great difficulty in obtaining it, and left that matter over till the next morning.

After breakfast she sought out Mr. Borrodaile and accosted him somewhat abruptly with the question, "What's Beresford Caldecott's address?"

"The amiable gentleman lives at Gradesleigh Hall, Rugby," said Mr. Borrodaile. "But what do you want to know for?"

"I have written to him," said the Lady Noggs, and with modest pride she drew the rough draft of the letter from her pocket and gave it to him.

Mr. Borrodaile took it with an expression of

dismay, and began to struggle with its perusal. Half-way through it he turned away from the Lady Noggs, and she gathered from the shaking of his back that he was a prey to some violent emotion. But when he had read it, he turned to her with a composed face, though there were tears in his eyes, and said, "I'm afraid you were misnamed, Noggs."

"What do you mean?" said the Lady Noggs.

"You ought to have been called Alexander or Archibald."

"Are you being funny?" said the Lady Noggs with extreme suspicion.

"No, no," said Mr. Borrodaile. "Alexander was the man who cut the Gordian knot; and Archibald was the gentleman who belled the cat."

"I don't know what you mean," said the Lady Noggs. "But I am going to send it anyhow — so there."

"Oh! send it, send it," said Mr. Borrodaile. "It can't do any harm; and I should say that it will probably have a brightening effect upon existence."

"That's what I thought," said the Lady Noggs. "And you won't be able to say you are down any more."

With that she left him, bolted to the school-room and addressed the letter before Miss Caldecott joined her. She posted it that afternoon when she went for her ride.

That afternoon, too, Mr. Borrodaile found Miss Caldecott and the duchess taking tea under the chestnut trees, on the edge of the big lawn, one of the largest stretches of old cultivated turf in England, and joined them. He seemed to have recovered his old habitual lightness of spirit; a recovery which it must be admitted, gave Miss Caldecott no great pleasure.

Presently he said, "Have you heard of the intervention of Noggs?"

"What intervention?" said the duchess.

"She has intervened in the matter at issue between Violet and myself," said Mr. Borrodaile.

"How?" said the duchess.

"Oh," said Mr. Borrodaile, "that's a secret," and he laughed with an exquisite enjoyment of the secret, very tantalizing to the curious.

"I insist upon your telling me, William; for the matter is in my hands," said the duchess.

"And it could not be in better," said Mr. Borrodaile with entirely hypocritical warmth. "But I'm afraid I cannot tell you, because, as I say, the intervention is Noggs's private affair."

There was no weakening his resolve to be silent, though the duchess exhausted command, adjuration, and entreaty in the effort. Her weapons had barely fallen blunted from the armour of his reserve, when the Lady Noggs herself appeared on the scene; but before the duchess could get in a question, the treacherous Mr. Borrodaile said, "I have just been telling them, Noggs, that you have been trying to help Violet and me, but the way you did it is a secret."

The hint was quite enough for the Lady Noggs; she nodded her head and said gravely, "Yes; it's a secret."

The duchess, dear soul, had not that full acquaintance with the Lady Noggs which the two others enjoyed, and she began to question her. But the Lady Noggs with a little help from Mr. Borrodaile grew vague and mysterious, and she got nothing out of her. In the end the duchess came to the conclusion that, after all, the intervention of the Lady Noggs could not be of any importance, though, merely as a matter of curiosity she would have liked to learn what it had been. She said, "Well, I hope it's all right. But Beresford is and always has been the worst-tempered man in the world." And she let the matter drop.

The Lady Noggs had made up her mind that the answer to her letter would come by post; and when next afternoon, she was walking on the lawn with Miss Caldecott, and a ramshackle, Warlesden cab disgorged a gentleman in a check suit, she did not connect him with her diplomatic missive. She was the more surprised when Miss Caldecott, who was walking with her, cried in a tone of the liveliest dismay, "Oh, dear! There's my uncle!"

"Is that your uncle?" said the Lady Noggs, looking earnestly at the man in the check suit, who was standing on the steps outside.

Then a footman came to the door, and she heard the visitor say, "I want to see Lady Felicia Grandison."

Plainly the footman pointed her out to him, for he strode down the steps and came towards them. The nearer he came the plainer grew the checks, until, when he was close to them, they obscured the man. The Lady Noggs tried hard to keep her eyes on his face, but the checks drew them away from it to themselves, strive as she might. However, she perceived that it was uncommonly red.

When he was quite close to them he put a glass into his eye, and said in a very fierce but jerky voice, "It's Violet! What! The idiot told me that Lady Felicia Grandison was on the lawn. It's her I want. I've come to say a few words about meddling with the affairs of other people to Lady Felicia Grandison — I want to tell her to mind her own business. What! Where is she, Violet? Eh! Where is she?"

"I'm here," said the Lady Noggs. "I'm Lady Felicia Grandison."

Mr. Caldecott turned his eyes quickly upon her, and a sudden blankness filled his face. "Eh, what! You're Lady Felicia Grandison?" and he looked at Violet for confirmation.

Violet nodded and said, "Yes, this is Lady Felicia Grandison."

Mr. Caldecott's red face went a good deal redder, and there poured from his lips a most impressive, continuous, but fortunately unintelligible stream of beautiful, sibilant, Spanish words mixed with such English expressions as "Sold again!" All this way for a kid! A blooming kid!" and like phrases. The gist of them was that he had made a mistake. He ended by turning on Violet and crying furiously, "Who put her up to it? Did you?"

"You know I didn't," said Violet coldly.

"Nobody put me up to it," said the Lady

Noggs. "I did it all myself, and I shall do it again if I want to; so it's no use you're being noisy."

"Noisy! Noisy!! Noisy!!!" cried Mr. Caldecott with a rising noisiness so that on the last word the cabman stood up anxiously on the box and the footman hurried out on to the steps in time to see the chequered visitor take off his pot-hat, throw it on the ground, and leap upon it with an accurate nimbleness, somewhat rare in a man of his years as there flowed from him once more a stream of beautiful, sibilant, Spanish words. The stream stopped suddenly, he kicked his shapeless hat, the luckless victim of his wrath, as far from him as he could.

Miss Caldecott looked frightened out of her wits, and tried to put the Lady Noggs behind her. The Lady Noggs wriggled out of her grasp, and watched this uncommon specimen of the English gentleman with the smiling appreciation he deserved. His hat and his Spanish seemed to have relieved him a little, for he drew an handkerchief from his pocket and mopped his fevered brow. Then he looked furiously round the lawn and said, "Hats are no use to me! I don't give a damn for hats!" And so saying, he drew from his pocket a neatly folded, grey checked silk cap, and put it on his head.

"You'd better come and have some tea, uncle," said Miss Caldecott with nervous haste.

"Eh, what? Tea! Tea! Tea! Eh, what? Tea!" said her uncle; and he laughed horridly.

"Yes," said Miss Caldecott. "It's at the other end of the lawn."

"Tea!" said her uncle hoarsely. "Well, I want to get to the bottom of this matter! I want to hear all about it! I want a word with that jackanapes, Borrodaile!" and he glared fiercely round the lawn, like a wolf looking for a lamb.

The look of apprehension on Miss Caldecott's face deepened; but she knew her uncle too well to say anything against that purpose; and she led the way towards the tea-table.

The Lady Noggs came round to the other side of Mr. Caldecott. "It must be expensive," she said thoughtfully.

"Eh, what? Expensive!" said Mr. Caldecott.

"Those hats," said the Lady Noggs.

Mr. Beresford Caldecott made a noise in his throat which might have been Aztec, but was certainly not beautiful, sibilant Spanish.

The Lady Noggs slipped her hand into Mr. Caldecott's, and said in a low, confidential voice not meant for the ears of his niece, "I rather like you — I've never seen any one jump on a hat before. I think you're awfully funny."

Mr. Beresford Caldecott stopped short with a gasp. "Funny!" he hissed. "Funny! and they called me Tiger Jake in Arizona!"

The Lady Noggs gave him a little tug which brought him along, and said, "Did they really? Tiger Jake — that's a splendid name. You looked like a tiger when you jumped on your hat."

Mr. Caldecott's eyes rolled painfully, but he found no words.

The duchess and Lady Hartlepool were sitting under a chestnut tree drinking their tea. At the sight of Mr. Caldecott the duchess opened her eyes, round and wide, and with extreme coldness, "Ah! Beresford! How do you do?" and held out her little finger.

Mr. Caldecott looked at it with some ungraciousness, and put both hands in his pockets: "It's all your fault, Elizabeth! What!" he said with aggressive bitterness. "Entirely your fault, and you know it! It was you, who put this nonsensical notion of earning her own living into Violet's head. What!"

"No, no, uncle," said Violet.

Mr. Caldecott was on the instant in another fury: "I tell you she did!" he roared glaring at the duchess. "I knew Elizabeth before you were born! What! She was interfering then, and she's interfering now! And look what comes of it! Here I am dependent on paid help, when I've a niece in the world who ought to be looking after me! What?"

"Have you any paid help?" said the duchess with cold unkindness. "I thought no servant ever stayed three days at Gradesleigh."

Mr. Caldecott grabbed for his hat. It was not there, and its absence seemed to confuse him, for he stood gasping.

The duchess took advantage of the pause to say, "Mr. Beresford Caldecott, the Marquess of Hartlepool."

"His name's not really Beresford, its Tiger Jake; he's just told me," said the Lady Noggs eagerly. "Isn't it a splendid name?"

At the sound of it, Mr. Caldecott drew himself up with an air.

"I don't know about it being splendid, but it certainly suits him," said the duchess unkindly. "Sit down, and have tea, Beresford."

"Tea! Tea!" said Beresford Caldecott with a horrid laugh. "No, thank you! I'm not here to drink tea! What? I want a young jackanapes called Borrodaile!"

"I'll go and tell him," said the Lady Noggs with gracious readiness. She was indeed eager to bring Mr. Borrodaile and this interesting new acquaintance together.

"Sit down, Noggs, and have your tea!" said the duchess and Miss Caldecott and Lady Hartlepool with one voice.

"Wilkins, bring some whisky and soda," said the duchess to one of the footmen who were waiting on them.

"Water! Water!" cried Mr. Caldecott, with fresh fury at the suggestion. "None of your beastly gas for me! What?"

He spent the time till the whisky came, in suppressing all attempts at conversation on the part of every one but the Lady Noggs. She made him nearly as uncomfortable as he made every one else, by asking, and indeed pressing home the question with extreme firmness, how he had earned his splendid name of Tiger Jake.

He did indeed assure her with every appearance of fury that "A little girl should be seen and not heard!" But his enunciation of this aphorism, to her the merest platitude, did not prevent her from inquiring whether he owed that glorious title to his appearance, his nature, his manners, or merely to some extraordinary piece of good fortune.

His yielding to her pertinacity so far as to roar furiously at her, "I was a bad man — a tough! What?" did not bring him relief from her questions, but only started her on an inquiry into the constitution of a "tough."

The coming of the whisky proved something of a diversion. The footman who was pouring it into a tumbler stopped at a liberal measure, but Mr. Caldecott sprang up with a little burst of beautiful, sibilant Spanish, snatched the bottle from him and trebled the quantity. Then, loudly as he had bawled for water, he made the very smallest use of it. He sat down again holding the tumbler in a hand on which there were but three fingers, since it is impossible to acquire such a filling and resounding title as Tiger Jake, and at the same time keep all your fingers; and he used that tumbler of whisky as a shield against the Lady Noggs. Whenever she asked him a question, he put it to his lips and held it there firmly, till the time for answering had gone by.

He had nearly got to the bottom of the tumbler when the duchess started, arose, and walked quickly to meet Mr. Borrodaile, who was coming briskly towards the tea-table.

"Eh! What? Stop!" roared Mr. Caldecott jumping out of his chair. "That's Borrodaile! I know it's Borrodaile! I want to say a few words to Borrodaile!"

The duchess stopped; and Mr. Borrodaile who had heard his name uttered very distinctly by a stranger, came up with an expression of polite enquiry on his face.

"You're Borrodaile! I know you're Borrodaile!" roared Mr. Caldecott.

"You're quite right," said Mr. Borrodaile, with a somewhat bewildered air, "though you do shout."

"Shout! I'm going to shout! What? I want a few words with you!" roared Mr. Caldecott. "My name's Caldecott, Beresford Caldecott! If you've got anything to say, say it at once! This moment! What?"

A light of recognition shone in Mr. Borrodaile's eyes, and he said, "What about?"

"Don't attempt to deny it!" said Mr. Caldecott. "I know the ways of skunks like you! Skunks, I say! You've been trifling with my niece's affections! It's no good your denying it! What?" and his voice rose to drown Mr. Borrodaile's protest. "You've been trifling with her affections! I won't hear a word! You thought she was an orphan and alone in the world! What?"

Mr. Borrodaile had been watching the foaming uncle with very shrewd eyes; suddenly he roared rather louder than Mr. Beresford Caldecott, "Don't you try to bully me, sir! I'm not to be bullied! you're in a land of law and order — not in some South American saloon!"

Mr. Beresford Caldecott's eyes seemed likely to burst out of his head and fly at Mr. Borrodaile; he wrung his hands, and danced a little dance of extreme nervous fury: "A land of law and order! Law and order!" he gasped hoarsely. "A South American saloon! Oh, if I'd got you in one! Oh, lord! What?"

"It would be absurd of Miss Caldecott and me to marry! Absurd!" Mr. Borrodaile shouted at him. "We can't afford it! And we're not going to be bullied into it by any bunco-steering broncho-buster from the wide pampas! No: we're not!" He was rather proud of his sonorous American, though he did not know what the words meant.

Their effect was soothing in a very curious way. They seemed to cool down Beresford Caldecott to a really murderous cold fury. Thrice his hands went round to his hip pocket and jerked back in two curious swift movements before he realized that it held no revolver. Then with a sighing gasp, and with a curious un-English high intonation he said, "Bunco-steering? Bunco-steering? Young feller, yew're goin' t' marry my niece inside of the month, or I'll shoot you up good and full. I'm not taking any of this talk about pauperism. I'm going straight to my lawyer, and he's going to fix it up that Violet gits ten thousand dollars a year right now. And if yew ain't married inside this month, as I says, I'll shoot you up good and full — law and order, or no law an' order." He cinched the proposition with an oath so elaborate and circumstantial that the three women turned pale to hear it; swung round, and walked off to his cab.

They looked after him without a word, till he reached it; then the duchess said with a shiver, "Well, I've never seen any one look like murder before, but I did then — absolute murder."

"He meant it — and he means it. Oh, why did you provoke him?" said Miss Caldecott turning to Mr. Borrodaile; and she wrung her hands, trembling. "What are we to do? — Whatever are we to do?"

"He meant it without a doubt; and I'm quite sure that he will fulfil his promise," said Mr. Borrodaile coolly. "But after all the life-saving process is easy."

"How? What process?" said Violet.

"The process of getting married before the end of the month. I must really call on you to save my life from your bloodthirsty relatives," said Mr. Borrodaile.

Miss Caldecott's paleness decreased with a remarkable swiftness, and she stammered, "Oh, well — of course — there is that way — but before the end of the month — how could I get ready?"

"I'll help you," said Mr. Borrodaile cheerfully.

"And I'll be a bridesmaid," said the Lady Noggs.

CHAPTER THIRTEEN

AN INFORMAL INTRODUCTION

IT was all pure goodness of heart; and no one was really to blame but the Prime Minister himself. If the Lady Noggs had not heard him bemoaning to Mr. Borrodaile the loss of time and the boredom he was enduring from the needless visit of Lord Grasthwaite, his senile but thick-witted President of the Board of Trade, she would never have cast about how to help him, and hit upon the ingenious device of applying an apple-pie bed to that minister by way of a hint that his stay at Stonorill had lasted long enough. Moreover, she considered an apple-pie bed a thing of little account, a pleasant form of humour easily appreciated and enjoyed by any one.

When, therefore, Lord Grasthwaite prefaced his breakfast by a bitter complaint of the discomfort he had endured from her effort to be helpful to her uncle, she was shocked alike by his tale-bearing and his lack of humour. But when the Prime Minister said in a tone of angry distress, "This is your doing, Felicia! go to the nursery and stay there for the rest of the day," surprise gave way to indignation.

She went out of the room with her head high, and a flush on her face; and, as she passed him, she gave the President of the Board of Trade a look of whole-hearted scorn which pierced even his second but confirmed childishness. Her indignation soon waxed to a righteous anger; injustice she could not endure; and it was grossly unjust that she should be punished for a well-meant effort to relieve her uncle of an incubus, and for the inability of a Cabinet Minister to see a joke.

Her anger grew and grew as the smart of her wounded dignity made the injustice clearer; and since with her to be angry was to act, she resolved on vengeance. She changed quickly into a 'holland frock, put her purse, containing four shillings into her pocket, and ready for flight, sat down and wrote painfully a hasty note; it ran:

Lady Felicia Grandison presents her complements to Lord Grasswaith and I think you are a horrid sneek.

She set this note on the dressing-table in Lord Grasthwaite's bedroom, ran down a flight of back stairs, and slipped out of a side door, just as Miss Caldecott, prevented by the Prime Minister from taking measures earlier, on the ground that paying too much attention to the child spoiled her, hurried into the empty nursery.

The Lady Noggs went out into the world with a high and indignant heart. Her immediate thought was vengeance, vengeance on her uncle for his unfairness; and her vengeance was to take the form of running away. She had been used to protest against injustice by a dignified retirement to a hiding-place on the wooded bank of the long pool at the end of the lawn. But this was too serious a matter, the injustice had been too public for so mild a protest. She said in her vengeful heart: "They *will* be sorry when I never, *never* come back!"

She ran down the shrubberies along the sides of the lawns, gained the home wood, and eased her pace to a walk; but it was a brisk walk. Then her vague purpose of running away began to assume more definite shape. The burden of her thought was: "Boys run away when they're ill-treated, why shouldn't girls?" And her small but active brain began to collect from memories of many story-books the methods pursued by the robuster sex in their flights. At the end of a con-

sideration which lasted two miles, it was clear
to her that the practice was to become a cabin-
boy and be wrecked on a desert island. This
course had the sanction of nearly all the authori-
ties.

She was now confronted with the question
how to become a cabin-boy; and here the au-
thorities left her, the burden of devising a method fell on her own wits. Her brow grew puckered, and insensibly she slackened her pace as she
wrestled with the difficulty. She tried to hope
that she might become a cabin-girl; but no
racking of her memory supplied her with an in-
stance of that responsible post having been filled
by a girl. It was plain that she must become a
boy. The difficulties in the way of this necessary transformation were her hair and clothes.
She resigned herself, not without a pang, to the
thought of cropping her hair; but the matter of
clothes was far more serious; she even took her
purse from her pocket, and gazed thoughtfully
at the four shillings in it. She shook her head
sadly: it was not enough. She fell to pondering
how to get money, and here she was indeed at a
loss. At last she was driven to dismiss the matter
firmly from her mind: the thing to do was to get
to the sea; it would be time enough then to set

about procuring clothes. This postponement of
the difficulty cheered her greatly; she was sure
that at the right moment the clothes of a cabin-
boy would come to hand — in her life most of
the things she had desired had come to hand —
and she went on more briskly.

At the end of the Stonorill woods she had
passed into the Beauleigh woods, and was pressing on straight through them. She knew that
England was an island, and if you walked
straight enough and far enough you must come
to the sea. When once she was out of her own
neighbourhood, and no longer known, she
would ask the nearest way to it. Half-way
through the Beauleigh woods she rested, and
found that she was exceedingly hungry; the loss
of her breakfast was telling, and she wished that
she had had time to raid the larder before starting. She was feeling a little faint when she reached the village of Appleton on the edge of the
Beauleigh woods, and the meal she made at the
village baker's was not only grateful, but restoring.

After it she went through the village, and took
a winding lane which leads away from Stonorill.
She had not yet asked the nearest way to the sea;
she was still too near her own country. She had

lost the vengeful feeling inspired into her by the outrage of her dignity; the spirit of adventure filled her to the exclusion of everything else; and since adventures are to the adventurous, she came straight to one. She had gone more than a mile down the lane, when she heard round a bend in front of her the crying of a kitten. She broke into a run, and came round the corner to find two fat, pasty-faced boys on the grass by the roadside, one of them sitting down and holding the protesting kitten, while he directed the operations of the other who was busy with an arrangement of sticks, string, and bobbins.

"What are you doing with that kitten?" said the Lady Noggs, coming to the point with her wonted directness.

The boy who was at work, looked up with a rapt air and said: "We're the Inquisition, and it's a heretic. When I've made this, we're going to put it to the question."

"How? What question?" said the Lady Noggs.

"I'm making a rack to stretch it on till it confesses its heresies." He spoke with enthusiasm.

"I think it's very cruel!" cried the Lady Noggs hotly.

"No one cares what you think," said the

other boy. "You get on! We don't want any little girls messing about here."

"Well, you're not going to, anyhow!" said the Lady Noggs. And on the words she darted forward, with a deft snatch caught up the kitten, and bolted down the road.

The boys were fat, and slow starting; but once started they began to catch her up. They had a long chase before they overtook her; and then she stood at bay with her back to the hedge.

"I'm — going — to give you — a jolly — good licking," panted the first inquisitor.

"We'll — teach you — to interfere," said the other; and they advanced on her with doubled fists.

The Lady Noggs did not double her fists; her fighting tactics were of a more open and feminine kind, and she kept her fingers free. The upshot was that she got some of those free fingers firmly gripped in the bigger boy's hair, and as he staggered about trying to unfasten them, and weakly protesting that the Queensbery rules were the only admissible method of fighting, she kicked the other boy's shins in the most womanly fashion.

This was all very well for a beginning, but the odds were too heavy against her; defeat was only a matter of a few minutes, when heaven declared against the big battalions. A motor-car came buzzing round the corner, stopped in about three times it's own length, and a clear voice cried: "Here! Stop this! What's it all about?"

The combatants stopped fighting, and turned to see a small boy standing in front of them, and regarding them with a judicial sternness. A little girl, a very fair, frail child, sat in the motor-car.

"What are you doing?" said the small boy again, with unabated firmness.

"They wanted to hurt the kitten, and I ran off with it!" cried the Lady Noggs with panting fierceness.

"Quite right," said the small boy.

"Then they said they were going to give me a jolly good licking," said the Lady Noggs.

"Well, you are cowardly cads — two fat boys to one little girl!" said the small boy with infinite scorn.

The epithet "fat," so wounding for its truth, collected the scattered wits of the inquisitors. They observed that this second intruder was younger and slighter than themselves; the delicate features of his seraph's face, and his uncommon cleanliness were plain marks of effeminacy; and with one voice they cried: "Look here, don't you interfere, or you'll get a licking yourself!"

"Shall I?" said the small boy quietly, and his sunny blue eyes turned grey and wary.

"Yes; you will," said the stouter of the inquisitors. "So just you look out!"

"Shall I come and help to lay them out with a spanner, Tinker?" said the gentle voice of the fair, frail child in the car; and she was standing up with a singularly robust specimen of that useful tool in her hand.

"No," said Tinker to her sharply, and then to the Lady Noggs "Get into the car!"

On his words the Lady Noggs bolted for the car with her usual promptness, and was in it before the inquisitors knew that she had started.

"Right away, Elsie! And wait further on!" cried Tinker; but the fair, frail child, used to the manœuvre, had started the car before he spoke.

The stout inquisitors dashed for it. Tinker tripped one as he rushed past him, turned swiftly, sprang on the other's back, and bore him to the ground. He had caught the moving car, and was tumbling into it, before they were on their feet. In a very natural fury they ran, shouting, to the end of their breath, before they grasped the fact that the car must be a good mile ahead of them, and adding at least three hundred yards a minute to that distance.

The car ran three miles before Elsie slowed down and stopped it. Then its passengers examined one another with the all-absorbing eyes of children which miss so little; and probably for the first time in her life, when Elsie threw aside her dust-cloak, and revealed a charming costume of muslin and lace which matched admirably her frail fairness, the Lady Noggs was afflicted with a slight discomfort at the though of her crumpled frock and dishevelled air. After a brief but searching scrutiny they turned their attention to the kitten. It seemed none the worse for its encounter with the Inquisition. Having assured themselves of its well-being, Tinker turned to the Lady Noggs, and said: "I'm Hildebrand Anne Beauleigh, and this is my sister— my adopted sister, Elsie Brand."

"I'm Lady Felicia Grandison," said the Lady Noggs.

Tinker bowed and said: "I'm charmed to meet you. But aren't you a long way from Stonorill?"

"I'm running away — running away to sea," said the Lady Noggs.

The faces of her new acquaintances brightened with the liveliest interest; but Tinker's tone
was a little doubtful as he said: "To sea?"

"Yes," said the Lady Noggs firmly. "Uncle
was awfully nasty to me this morning; and he
told me before everybody at breakfast to go to
the nursery and stay there all day, just because I
made an apple-pie bed for Lord Grasthwaite,
and he sneaked. And I won't be scolded before
everybody. Would you?"

A faint, retrospective smile brightened Tinker's face as he said: "It sometimes happens."

"Well, but it wasn't fair as well," the Lady
Noggs protested. "I only made the apple-pie
bed for Lord Grasthwaite just to show him that
he'd stayed long enough. Uncle doesn't like him
to stay at Stonorill; he bores him to extinction. I
don't know what extinction is, but I heard him
say so; and it must be horrid. That's why I did
it; and it isn't fair I should be scolded for it."

"It's very hard to do anything for grown-
ups," said Tinker. "They're scarcely ever
thankful."

"Well, anyhow, it wasn't fair, and I'm going
to run away to sea, and dress up and be a cabin-
boy," said the Lady Noggs firmly.

There was a short silence, as her companions

considered the scheme with the air of experts; then Tinker said: "I'm afraid it won't work. They won't have you for one thing, because they'll find out you're a girl."

"But they can't! I shall cut my hair off," said the Lady Noggs.

"You'll find it very hard not to cut it crooked; and it wouldn't look at all nice," said Elsie.

The Lady Noggs put up her hand to it with a sudden nervous gesture; but she said bravely: "Oh, I don't mind that."

"Yes;" but it isn't only not being found out," said Tinker. "But the sea isn't what it was. I've talked to cabin-boys; and it isn't at all a nice life. And it's so awfully hard to get shipwrecked nowadays — properly that is. There don't seem to be any desert islands left; and if you did get wrecked on one, some ship would come and take you off in about a month."

The Lady Noggs's face fell: "I never heard of that." she said.

"And the sea isn't good enough unless you do get shipwrecked properly on a desert island. It's jolly uncomfortable, and rough, and so dull, the same thing day after day. It's just the same whether you're on a steamer or a sailing-ship. I've talked to lots of cabin-boys — lots. And if you're not going to get a desert island out of it, what's the good of it?" said Tinker.

"Then the books aren't true," said the Lady Noggs in a sorrowful voice.

"I fancy they were true enough, some of them. But they're all about things that happened years and years ago. The sea's getting crowded, I think," said Tinker.

"Well, then, what is one to do, when people behave badly?" said the Lady Noggs with some indignation.

Tinker shrugged his shoulders. "You can't do anything," he said. "You just have to sit tight."

"But that's just what I don't want to do!" cried the Lady Noggs. "It wasn't fair."

"Things often aren't," said Tinker, with the air of a sage. "But the only thing to do is to sit tight, isn't it Elsie?"

"You have to," said Elsie.

"Of course, if you sit tight long enough, the time comes when you can make the other people sit up," said Tinker.

The Lady Noggs's face slowly brightened: "I could always do that, couldn't I?" she said. "I could make Lord Grasthwaite sit up."

"Then you won't run away to sea?" said Tinker.

"Not if there aren't any desert islands," said the Lady Noggs firmly.

"That's all right," said Tinker, with an air of real relief. "You wouldn't have liked it — really."

"But I'm not going straight home all the same — not till ever so late," said the Lady Noggs vengefully. "I'll let them hunt for me."

Tinker was silent. He seemed to be thinking hard. Then, with a bright, seraphic smile he said: "I'll tell you what, Elsie. I'm not a bit keen on going to the Harpendens. Mary Harpenden will be bothering all the afternoon. She'll very likely ask me to kiss her again, and I might feel, being a visitor and all that, that it wouldn't be quite nice to go on making excuses."

"I don't believe you really want to make any excuses. She's a horrid, forward little girl," said Elsie with some tartness.

"Now that is a silly thing to say. You know how I hate kissing people — every one but you, that is!" he added hastily.

"I think kissing's silly," said the Lady Noggs.

"So do I," said Tinker in warmest agreement.

"It depends who you kiss," said Elsie shortly.

"Now just listen," said Tinker earnestly. "I've thought of a way how Lady Grandison —"

"I'd rather you call me Noggs. Everybody —
all the people I like, that is — call me Noggs,"
interrupted the Lady Noggs.

" — how Noggs can score all round." Tinker
went on. "And I think it will be rather a game.
I'll be Raisuli; you know — the Morocco brig-
and. And you shall be my lieutenant; and she
shall be Miss Perdicaris. And we've kidnapped
her; and we'll keep her in the pavilion on the
hill, until her uncle pays her ransom."

"Oh, that will be fun!" said the Lady Noggs.
"When I don't come home to-night, uncle will be
sorry he wasn't fair!"

CHAPTER FOURTEEN

IN THE BRIGAND'S LAIR

ELSIE set the car going again, and turned down a side lane. About forty yards down it she steered the car on to the grass under the screen of the hedge, and stopped. They stood up while Tinker rummaged in the box under the cushion, and drew from it writing paper, none too clean, envelopes, and a pencil. He knelt down, and using the seat as a table, wrote, to all seeming with some pain, a letter which ran,

I have kidnaped your neece but she will not be hurt if you pay her randsome at once. My leftenant will come for it at 10 tomorow at the botom of the Stonnorrill drive. It is five hundred pounds in gold. Come alone.

THE ENGLISH RASULY.

He read it aloud, and said with natural pride, "I think that ought to work it."

"Rather," said Elsie. "And won't it be nice to have all that money?"

"We could get a new car. It would be awfully handy to have a car each," said Tinker. "We could do a lot more with two cars than with one."

"Couldn't we?" said Elsie. And their eyes seemed to light up with splendid visions of a yet further discomfited Humanity.

The Lady Noggs regarded them with admiring respect; but in a moment Tinker returned to the present earth, and said, "What we've got to do now is to get Noggs to the Pavilion on the hill without anybody seeing her."

For them it was no difficult matter. They arranged her sitting in the bottom of the car between them, with a light rug covering her to the chin, to be raised to hide her face and head when they should be passing any one; then they set out for Beauleigh. They stopped to post the letter in the first village they passed through, and in rather less than twenty minutes they went through the lodge gates into Beauleigh Park. Half-way across it they turned off to the left from the main drive, along a narrow road running up-hill through stretches of bracken broken by clumps of oak and fir.

They drove slowly, for the roadway was bad; and at the end of rather more than a mile of it they came over the brow of the ridge on to a plateau in the middle of which stood the Pavilion. It was a marble building in the pseudo-classic style affected by the polite of the Regency: a whim of the Beauleigh of that day. Once it had been all white; but creepers had been allowed to struggle patiently upwards over the unkindly marble till much of its whiteness was hidden by a veil of green. From all four sides its tall windows and its flat roof commanded an admirable view over the country round. In that flatter land, indeed, it had, as a brigand's lair, all the advantages of one of the old robber castles on German peaks.

The car stopped before the front door; and Tinker jumped out and opened it with his latch-key. They went into the hall and found it very cool and dark for the windows were shuttered. Tinker and Elsie set about opening the shutters and the windows on the sides on which the sun was not shining; then they turned their hospitable attention to the Lady Noggs. She was very thirsty after her flight from the inquisitors, and they were much put about that they could only at the moment give her water to drink. Tinker fetched it; and then he said, "If you don't mind waiting here alone Elsie and I will

make you some tea. We shall do it quicker together. We always keep tea and sugar, and
things like that here, because if it is a very hot
night we come up from the Court and sleep
here. It is so much cooler."

But the Lady Noggs begged to be allowed to
help them; and they all went to the kitchen.
Elsie and Tinker got the fire lighted with the
quickness of experts; and as soon as it was burning steadily, Tinker said, "Now, while the ket-
tle's boiling I'll ride down to the Court and
bring up some milk and cakes for tea; and I'll
tell them to send up food for dinner and breakfast later; only we must keep a lookout for
their coming, for it won't do for any one to see
Noggs."

"You'd better tell Selina to come up and
wait on us. She's quite safe," said Elsie.

"Yes, that will be most comfortable," said
Tinker.

They went to the door and saw him start;
then the Lady Noggs turned to Elsie, and said,
"Could I — could I have a bath?"

"If you don't mind a cold one," said Elsie.

"I want it cold," said the Lady Noggs. After
her tramp, and flight, and struggle with the inquisitors that was indeed her need; and Elsie

took her up to the bath-room. She insisted also, on providing her with a change of clothes, explaining that she always kept plenty of clothes there because they used the place so much. By the time she had bathed and dressed, and helped her hostess set out the tea-things Tinker was back with the milk and cakes.

When he saw the table arranged for tea he frowned a little, and said, "I'm afraid we can't sit up to tables. They don't in Morocco."

Accordingly the tea-things were transferred from the table to the floor, the table was put in a corner, cushions were set round the tea-things, and they took the meal sitting cross-legged on them in no very great comfort, but with infinite satisfaction to the scrupulous minds of Elsie and Tinker.

After tea they busied themselves making the room as Moroccan as possible. They carried out all the furniture except the couches, and brought in all the cushions they could find from the other rooms in the Pavilion. They were even so scrupulous as to remove, also, the pictures from the walls. In the middle of this sacrifice to accuracy, Elsie's maid Selina arrived: a middle-aged woman of a very rugged countenance. To the surprise of the Lady Noggs Tinker at once

informed her of the fact that she had been kidnapped, and was being held to ransom. The
Lady Noggs was even more surprised when
Selina made no protest, but only said with patient glumness, "I expect there'll be a fine to do
about it."

The truth was that Selina had been the nurse
of Tinker's babyhood, and was devoted to him.
The penalty of this devotion was that she had
to abet him in his operations under pain of his
displeasure. If she failed him that displeasure
took the form of banishing her for a week at a
time from the light of his presence. She went to
the kitchen to receive the provisions when they
should come up from the Court, and to prepare
their dinner.

Then Tinker and Elsie set themselves very
seriously to construct from a vague and general
knowledge of the East the probable manners
and customs of the too little known country
of Morocco. The Lady Noggs could not help;
she could only admire. As the evening advanced
these customs increased in number. They were
perhaps a little inexact in the matter of sitting
cross-legged, for they did not take kindly to the
attitude; and the casting of Selina for the part
of Mesrour gave rather an air of Bagdad than

of Morocco to the gathering. All through the evening Tinker was seriously Sultanesque; and Elsie had to play several parts. She had been definitely appointed the lieutenant of the English Raisuli under the name of Abdallah ben Ali; but she was at times also the Sultaness Scheherazade, and Zobeide the Kaliph's Lady. The Lady Noggs found the part of Miss Perdicaris the captive, somewhat monotonous, and was permitted to become the fair Persian, though as Tinker pointed out she ought not to have been dark, and various princesses of China, of Rajputana, and of islands impossible to find on any map.

For most of the evening the brooding calm of the East rested on them unbroken. Indeed, there was no one to intrude, for Sir Tancred and Lady Beauleigh were away from home. But now and again Tinker would remember that he was a brigand in a fastness; and they would go out and inspect the line of keen-eyed but imaginary sentries who watched over their safety. Twice on their round the English Raisuli paused to discuss with his trusty lieutenant the chances of a raid upon houses in the low-lying plain, whose foolish lights drew to them the attention of this scanty but nefarious band.

After a last inspection at nine o'clock they went to bed. The Lady Noggs awoke early and in the highest possible spirits: her new friends charmed her; and she was eager for their society. She had never before come across any one so nearly after her own heart. When she had made her toilet, with Selina's help in the matter of her hair, she went down-stairs to find Tinker and Elsie attending to the motor-car. When they had done, they went to breakfast; and over it they discussed the details of the collection of the ransom of five hundred pounds in gold. Tinker would have liked to play a double part, to be not only Raisuli but Raisuli's envoy; but in a generous spirit he allowed Elsie, as his trusty lieutenant Abdallah ben Ali, to have the honour of fetching that round sum. When he had, after discussion, arrived at this decision the Lady Noggs had a word to say: "It's all very well for them to send this five hundred pounds," she said. "But I'm not going back to Stonorill when it comes. I am going to stop here; that is, if you don't mind."

Tinker said with hasty politeness: "Oh! we should be awfully pleased to have you here." Then he knitted his brow over the problem so suddenly presented to him, and went on, "The only thing is, if your uncle pays your ransom we should be bound to return you to him."

"Not at once," said the Lady Noggs.

"Well, the same day, at any rate," said Tinker.

"Suppose," said Elsie with whole-hearted generosity. "Suppose, we don't ask for any ransom; but just keep Noggs here with us without saying anything about her. They'll be a long time finding out."

Tinker shook his head, and said firmly: "No; if you are Raisuli, you have to get ransoms."

"Yes, of course you do; I was forgetting," said Elsie.

"Well, if you do take me back to Stonorill it doesn't make any difference: I shall come back," said the Lady Noggs gloomily.

Tinker looked at her with a frowning thoughtfulness; then of a sudden his face cleared, and he said joyfully: "Yes, of course; if once you've been returned properly to your uncle, there's nothing to prevent your joining the band afterwards."

Having settled this point they discussed the course of action to be taken should anything go wrong with Elsie's mission; and it was arranged that if she had not returned by lunch time, when the Prime Minister should have had time, and to spare, to raise the five hundred pounds in gold, Tinker should come down to Stonorill in a horse drawn vehicle, and set about extricating her from whatever plight she might be in.

This final arrangement brought them to the end of breakfast, and they went out to the car. At the sight of it Tinker, meticulous in the matter of detail, became the prey to a sudden gloom: "You ought to go on a camel," he said, looking at it despitefully.

Elsie and the Lady Noggs looked at the car, and also felt that it was radically wrong. They were silent for a minute considering the discrepancy; then Elsie pointed out that after all it would excite less remark in the English lanes than that well-stomached animal.

"Yes, there is that," said Tinker; and then he added firmly: "Well, I tell you what, we'll consider it a camel. If you come to look at it, a motor-car is rather humpy."

Satisfied with this solution of the difficulty, Elsie proceeded to mount the motor-car in the fashion in which they suspected that a Moroccan mounted a camel; then off she went, full of her high emprise, and prepared to act with firmness and discretion.

Meanwhile the inhabitants of Stonorill Castle had passed an anxious night. They had not been anxious during the day, since they supposed that the Lady Noggs had followed her usual custom of retiring into hiding because her dignity had been ruffled. But at half-past eight in the evening they began to grow anxious; and by half-past nine they were anxious indeed. By a quarter to ten a band of searchers was exploring the grounds; and four mounted grooms were moving north, south, east, and west from Stonorill, inquiring at the villages they passed through. The search in the grounds proved fruitless, and by one in the morning all the four grooms had returned with the news that they had found no trace of the truant. It chanced that the Appleton baker, at whose shop she had made her midday meal, was sleeping soundly when the inquiring groom passed through that village. One of them had, however, ascertained that she had not gone by train from Warlesden.

On the return of these unsuccessful emissaries the Prime Minister took one motor-car; Mr. Borrodaile, accompanied by Miss Caldecott, took another; the Prime Minister's chauffeur took the third, and they set about exploring the country in a circle round Stonorill. After a fruitless search they came back to the castle about five o'clock in the morning, and thought it best to get a few hours sleep before starting upon a more thorough and elaborate search in the daylight. They had taken that few hours sleep, had risen and dressed, and were concerting measures for that thorough and elaborate search, when the postman came bringing Tinker's letter.

The Prime Minister was astounded by the revelation it contained of the audacious depravity of his quiet neighbourhood: "Dear, dear! this is very distressing!" he said. "In England! In the twentieth century!"

Mr. Borrodaile after examining the letter carefully, said, "It looks to me as if the English Raisuli were of tender years. I don't think we need call out the militia to deal with him; and I think we might, by the exercise of that diplomacy in which we are so skilled, beat down the ' randsome' a little."

"Ransom! You don't suppose I have any intention of deliberately encouraging blackmail by paying a ransom!" cried the Prime Minister.

"I can quite conceive you might have to," said Mr. Borrodaile drily. "Unless of course you could consent to forego the somewhat wearing delight of Lady Felicia's society for a week or two."

"Dear, dear! this is very distressing!" said the Prime Minister.

"Well, we can't do anything till we have conferred with the brigand's envoy," said Mr. Borrodaile. "So I suppose we may as well have breakfast at our leisure. After all, we know the most important thing, that no accident has happened to Nog — Lady Felicia. She's safe, at any rate."

During the breakfast the Prime Minister discussed at length with many hard words the unexpected depravity of his quiet neighbourhood. Mr. Borrodaile did not join in his diatribes. He was disposed to wait to see what the hour of ten brought forth.

At a quarter to ten the Prime Minister went down to the appointed place, accompanied by Mr. Borrodaile and two sturdy footmen, armed, by their own choice, with cricket stumps. These seemed to them the handiest weapons. They were posted in the lodge itself with instructions to rush out at the Prime Minister's signal. He himself with Mr. Borrodaile waited before the lodge door. At two minutes to ten there came the hoot of a motor horn, and a car buzzed round the corner up to the gates, and stopped. A very fair, frail child descended from it, saluted them in exact military fashion, and said in a charming voice, "The English Raisuli has sent me for that ransom — five hundred pounds in gold." And she held out her hand for the money.

The Prime Minister looked at her in frankly open-mouthed astonishment, thought of his two sturdy myrmidons waiting in the lodge with their cricket stumps, and blushed to the soles of his boots.

Mr. Borrodaile raised his hat and smiled: "I see that we owe the disappearance of Lady Grandison to the kindly attention of our young neighbours," he said. "I recognize your car."

"It's not a car; it's a camel," said Elsie firmly.

"Of course. How stupid of me!" said Mr. Borrodaile, affecting to regard the object more closely. "I mean your camel."

"Have you got the money?" said Elsie with simple directness.

"Really — really — this — this — early depravity is shocking! Do you know, little girl, that this is blackmailing — blackmailing?" stammered the Prime Minister.

"I don't know anything about blackmailing,

or what it is. I've come for the five hundred pounds in gold," said Elsie keeping to the point with womanly pertinacity.

The Prime Minister took hold firmly of his beard with both hands.

"Suppose we haven't brought the five hundred pounds in gold, and don't mean to pay it; what would happen?" said Mr. Borrodaile. And he stepped carelessly between Elsie and her mechanical camel.

She turned to him with knitted brow, and after a thoughtful pause said earnestly, "We haven't talked that over, Tinker and I, so I don't know quite. But Tinker would be sure to do what Raisuli generally does. He always likes to do things properly."

"Ah, he has a strong sense of the fitness of things, evidently," said Mr. Borrodaile. "Well, we're not going to pay any ransom. We're going to exchange prisoners instead. You're our prisoner; and we're going to exchange you for Lady Grandison."

A faint flush stained Elsie's pale fairness; she looked sharply round, and sprang for the car, only to land in Mr. Borrodaile's arms. He picked her up, carried her inside the park gates, and set her down. Then he folded his arms, assumed a melodramatic scowl; and said in the true transpontine manner, "Resistance is useless. I am going to take your car and drive straight to Beauleigh Court and bring back Lady Grandison."

With no great sighs of dismay Elsie straightened her hat and shook out her frock; then she looked round somewhat ruefully, and said, "You won't find her there."

"I've only to follow your wheel tracks," said Mr. Borrodaile. "They will take me to wherever she is."

Elsie looked at the thick dust on the drive, and saw that he spoke truly; but she only said, "You may not be able to do it."

"I think I shall," said Mr. Borrodaile. And turning to the Prime Minister he added, "I will leave the English Raisuli's envoy in your hands, sir."

The Prime Minister showed no enthusiasm at the prospect. He looked at Elsie glumly.

Mr. Borrodaile turned and went. As he passed through the gates of the Park, Elsie cried after him in a singularly discomfiting tone, "Mind the bloodhound!"

Mr. Borrodaile got into her car, and started; he followed the tracks of its wheels to Beauleigh

Park without any difficulty. He found that they ran into the park; but inside it he found that the drive was marked with several sets of tracks which had been undisturbed by other traffic for several days. At the road which turned off up to the Pavilion on the hill he stopped; then seeing that it had been used for motor traffic he made up his mind that he was very likely to find his quarry at the end of it. Accordingly he sent the car up it, and driving it carefully came at last to the little plateau on which stood the Pavilion. When he saw it, he was sure he had come to the right place.

Thanks to the admirable situation of the Pavilion, Tinker and the Lady Noggs had seen the car a mile away, and had long been aware that it was not driven by Elsie. At once they hurried up to the flat roof, Tinker carrying a pair of race-glasses. The Lady Noggs was some time getting them focussed on to the car; when she did, she cried, "It is that beast, Billy!"

Tinker was watching it with some anxiety: "It looks," he said, "as if they'd collared Elsie."

"It's just what they'd do!" said the Lady Noggs scornfully.

"Well, you stop up here," said Tinker, "and I'll go down, and talk to him."

Mindful of Elsie's parting admonition Mr. Borrodaile drove up to the Pavilion somewhat gingerly, casting a wary eye about him for bloodhounds. When he reached it he saw a small boy standing in the doorway, regarding him with the genuine brigand scowl.

"The English Raisuli, I believe," said Mr. Borrodaile.

The small boy nodded.

"Lord Errington had a letter from you, this morning, informing him that you had kidnapped his niece, Lady Felicia Grandison, and suggesting a ransom of five hundred pounds in gold. We met the envoy you sent to get the money at the appointed place, and captured her. I have come to propose an exchange of prisoners. We will surrender your envoy, if you will surrender Lady Grandison."

"Do you bear a token from my envoy to show that your story is true?" said Tinker in a very gruff voice.

"Token?" said Mr. Borrodaile a little blankly. "Oh, yes; here's her camel."

Tinker's face cleared somewhat at this concession to romance: "It is," he said gruffly.

"Well, where is Lady Grandison?" said Mr. Borrodaile.

"Up-stairs," said Tinker.

"Then I think if you will allow me, I'll come up-stairs and fetch her. She might refuse to come at your bidding. I know her well."

Tinker turned and led the way through the hall, and up the stairs. All the way he grumbled bitterly in a very gruff voice, about the unfairness of taking a mean advantage of a little girl like Elsie.

Mr. Borrodaile heard him without a word. He only suffered a triumphant smile to wreathe his face.

On the first floor landing Tinker turned the handle of a door and threw it wide open. Mr. Borrodaile composed his countenance to an expression likely to overawe the Lady Noggs, should she be unwilling to return with him. He was also making an impressive, overawing entrance; but it was spoiled by a vigorous push which sent him flying into the middle of the room. Before he could turn, the door was slammed, and the key turned in the lock.

"Ha, ha! Trapped!" said the gruff voice of the English Raisuli.

That resourceful but unscrupulous brigand went coolly up to the roof to the Lady Noggs.

A smile of gentle contentment played about his lips, and he said, "I've trapped him. He's locked up in the morning-room. That's two prisoners to one: they will learn that the English Raisuli is not to be trifled with."

"You've caught Billy and locked him up?" cried the Lady Noggs clapping her hands. "You *are* a nice boy. I *do* like you. But are you sure he can't get out?"

"There are no creepers near that window. That's why I chose the morning-room," said Tinker.

Mr. Borrodaile had already ascertained that fact. He had rushed straight to the window the moment the gruff voice of the English Raisuli had apprised him of his capture. Then he sat down in an arm-chair and laughed. Presently he again set about trying to find some method of escaping from the brigand's clutches. He went to the window and again examined the wall with a view to clambering down it. It was most inconvenient for any such purpose: a smooth twenty feet to the marble pavement of the terrace at its foot. He tried the door. It seemed to him of uncommon thickness, with an uncommonly strong lock. He betook himself to the examination of the fine coloured prints with which the room was most fittingly hung; then he went to the window again.

Two children, the English Raisuli and his prisoner, Lady Felicia Grandison, were walking on the terrace below it, in earnest and entirely amicable conversation.

"Hulloa!" cried Mr. Borrodaile.

Neither of them vouchsafed so much as a glance upwards. For half an hour they walked up and down underneath his window absorbed in their talk. Mr. Borrodaile made proposals; he was sarcastic; he even threatened. They might have been stone deaf for all the attention they paid to him. He gave it up at last, and settled himself, somewhat sulkily, in an arm-chair with a book.

Meanwhile things had been going no better in Stonorill park. After Mr. Borrodaile had left them, Elsie sat down on the grass. The Prime Minister stood over her and took the pains to point out to her at great length, and with that famous eloquence which had done almost as much as his family to raise him to his exalted position, the enormity of the crime of blackmailing.

When at last he came to the end of his harangue, Elsie only said, "Brigands do."

The Prime Minister then waited in silence. Presently the two footmen came somewhat sheepishly out of the lodge. They did not carry their cricket stumps. The Prime Minister told them to go back to the castle. Elsie's face brightened.

They waited on, still silent. The Prime Minister having exhausted the moral aspect of the matter, could find nothing to say to his prisoner; and she seemed to have nothing to say to him. It was quite a half an hour before a sudden happy thought came to him, and he said stiffly, "I can't waste any more time on the tiresome pranks of children; you may as well wait at the castle as here. Come along."

Elsie rose with ready obedience, and came. The motion, or the fresh air set the fine intellect of the Prime Minister wandering along the paths of German philosophy. It wandered in that perfect concentration only possible to great minds. At the end of three-quarters of a mile he bethought himself of his blackmailing companion, and cast a glance down on her. His eyes met the empty air. A glance around assured him that he was alone; a third glance, backwards, showed him a white figure moving at a considerable speed, rather more than half a mile away. He said something neither German nor philosophical, and started in pursuit. His legs were long but by no means used to the exercise of running, and he had made no perceptible gain on it when the white figure vanished out of sight through the park gates. He stopped short, sat down till he had recovered his breath; and then slowly and gloomily went towards the castle.

When it became plain that Mr. Borrodaile was not coming again to the window to be annoyed by their contemptuous disregard of him, Tinker and the Lady Noggs left the terrace. The sight of the motor-car gave him an idea. He pulled out his watch, looked at it, made a short calculation, and said, "I think I ought to be getting down to Stonorill: Elsie's been there more than an hour, and if your uncle's anything like what you tell us, I'll bet anything she's got away by now. She's used to it. We're both used to it. I think, if you don't mind being left alone, I ought to be getting down to Stonorill in case she wants me."

"Can't I come with you?" said the Lady Noggs.

"I don't think you'd better," said Tinker. "It's all right for me; I'm pretty hard to catch, especially in a ca — on a camel."

The Lady Noggs's face fell; then it brightened, and she said, "But you could cover me with a rug like you did yesterday."

"Yes, I could do that," said Tinker somewhat doubtfully. "But suppose we had to leave the car and run for it."

"Oh, I can run all right," said the Lady Noggs. "And we should be near the woods, too; and when once I get into the woods, I know of lots and lots of hiding-places where they'd never find me. And I do so want to come."

"Well, we might try," said Tinker with no great enthusiasm.

Accordingly the Lady Noggs was again arranged in the bottom of the car so that she could be covered with a rug, and Tinker started the car down the hill. On the level ground he made it fly, and kept up the pace to within a mile of Stonorill; then he slowed down, and advanced on the castle with great caution. Several times he got out of the car and looked round the corner of the road or over the brow of a ridge in it. They were approaching a corner in this cautious fashion, not above half a mile from the lodge gates, when there came flying round it a little white figure with streaming hair. At the sight of it Tinker cheered, the Lady Noggs clapped her hands, and in a few seconds the panting Elsie was in the car, and it was ripping back to Beauleigh.

Some half an hour after this incident Mr. Borrodaile went to the window to see if anywhere in the surrounding country a rescuer was speeding towards him. The surrounding country was painfully empty; but on the terrace immediately beneath him walked three children, two little girls and a boy; they were absorbed in earnest conversation. Mr. Borrodaile stared a moment with all his eyes, said something in a low voice and sprang away from the window hoping that he had not been seen. He went back to his arm-chair and his book a subdued and chastened man. He read with no very great gusto for some time; then of a sudden he became aware that he was hungry. The discovery soon made him hungrier; and the improbability of satisfying that hunger was both plain and painful to him. He rose and went again to the window. The terrace was empty, and he scanned the surrounding country wistfully. He knew the Prime Minister too well to hope that he would have moved so soon in the matter of his rescue. Of a sudden he heard steps outside the door; and the key turned in the lock. Mr.

Borrodaile strode hurriedly across the room resolved to be free. On the landing stood the English Raisuli, and by his side a maid bearing a
lunch tray; on the threshold stood an admirable
specimen of the brindled bull-terrier: he seemed
to Mr. Borrodaile to be displaying several rows
of long, sharp teeth. Mr. Borrodaile stopped
short.

"This is Blazer the bloodhound," said the
English Raisuli with a complacency which Mr.
Borrodaile found excessive. "If you try to come
out of the room, he will tear you limb from
limb."

Mr. Borrodaile disbelieved in the dog's breed,
but not in his rending powers; and he stood still.

"Take in the lunch, Selina," said the English
Raisuli; and he folded his arms and regarded
his captive with a stern and gloomy frown.

The maid brought in the tray and set it on
the table; then she went out of the room, and
the English Raisuli shut the door, and turned
the key. Mr. Borrodaile again said a word or
two in a low voice; then he got him to his lunch.
Fortunately he had cigarettes with him, and
after his lunch he smoked a couple; then he
turned drowsy and went to sleep. He was aroused
by the sound of banging; he looked at his watch

and found that he had slept nearly two hours; then he perceived that the banging which had aroused him, was the sound of doors and shutters being closed hastily. He sprang to the window to see, as he expected, the Prime Minister accompanied by his chauffeur, coming on to the plateau in his motor-car. Mr. Borrodaile shouted, but just too late; for the car passed the corner of the Pavilion on its way to the front door. It was some five minutes before the Prime Minister and the chauffeur came round the corner.

"I'm glad you've come!" cried Mr. Borrodaile. "I've been a prisoner here since eleven this morning!"

"Dear, dear! this is very distressing!" said the Prime Minister. "But how has it happened? Who has imprisoned you?"

"That young imp, Sir Tancred Beauleigh's son," said Mr. Borrodaile.

"But how are we to get in? How are we to release you?" said the Prime Minister. "Except for you the building seems deserted. The door is shut and all the windows are shuttered."

"Break in," said Mr. Borrodaile. "You've plenty of tools in the car; and Gavroche knows how to use them."

"But how can I break into a house — a deserted house?" said the Prime Minister plaintively.

"It isn't deserted," said Mr. Borrodaile. "Lady Felicia is in it, and two Beauleigh children, and at any rate one maid; to say nothing of a bull terrier."

"Bloodhound," said a hoarse brigand-like voice from the roof. And Mr. Borrodaile and the Prime Minister looked up to see no one.

"I was forgetting that dog," said Mr. Borrodaile. "He complicates matters. He'll be more awkward to deal with than a man; but it's the only thing to do."

The Prime Minister paced the terrace in an agony of indecision. The chauffeur watched him stolidly. At last the Prime Minister said, "Well, there really seems to be nothing else to do; but it's very distressing! very distressing! Where do you suggest that I shall break in?"

"The front door if you can manage it," said Mr. Borrodaile. "But I expect you will have to fight that dog."

"There is no need at all to break in," said the gruff voice of the brigand from the roof. "If you've brought that five hundred pounds in gold, the captives will be released at once. If you try to break in, beware of Blazer the blood-hound and the molten lead."

The Prime Minister again scanned the parapet of the roof, but again he saw no brigand. Suddenly, by a splendid effort, he came to a definite resolve: "Look here, Borrodaile," he said, "I'm not going to break in. Suppose Felicia isn't in the house. I should get into a horrible mess. Sir Tancred Beauleigh would be justified in prosecuting me. Think of what the papers would say."

"But if Lady Felicia isn't here, I'm here," said Mr. Borrodaile.

"You came in of your own accord," said the voice of the brigand.

"That's true, you know, that's quite true," said the Prime Minister. "I shall drive over to Wyse's and get a search-warrant, and a policeman to do things in the regular way."

"By the time you get back, Raisuli and his prey will be far away," said the voice of the brigand.

"Dear, dear! This is very distressing!" said the Prime Minister, once more at a loss.

Of a sudden help, unexpected but effective, came. A tall, slim, young man came slowly round the back of the Pavilion along the terrace.

He showed no surprise at all at the sight of a stranger conversing, from a first-floor window of his Pavilion, with an agitated Prime Minister. He only said with languid politeness, "I fear that you must have come across my small son. I am Sir Tancred Beauleigh."

The Prime Minister bowed with some stiffness, since before his recent marriage with an American heiress Sir Tancred had enjoyed the reputation of being something of a ne'er-do-well, and said with some heat, "I have indeed, at least I think so. He has kidnapped my little niece, and proposed to blackmail me — actually to blackmail me — by holding her to ransom."

"I can well believe it," said Sir Tancred with languid coolness, for the Prime Minister's stiffness had not escaped his notice.

"Then on the top of that, he has imprisoned Mr. Borrodaile, my secretary!"

"Ah, the gentleman in my morning-room. Doesn't he look rather large to be imprisoned by a small boy like Tinker?"

"Oh, I was fairly trapped," said Mr. Borrodaile. "I have nothing to complain of. I came as an enemy, and I followed our national custom of despising the enemy, with the result that I got into trouble. It served me quite right."

"Well, we will hear what Tinker has to say about himself. I have never yet found him unprovided with admirable reasons for these exploits," said Sir Tancred.

"Am I to understand that you propose to encourage him in this outrageous conduct?" cried the Prime Minister with yet more heat.

"I propose to keep my mind quite open," said Sir Tancred with a charming smile. "After all, the presence of your secretary in my morning-room does require some explanation."

The Prime Minister found nothing to say; and Sir Tancred shouted up to the roof, "Tinker."

The head of the English Raisuli appeared over the parapet, and Sir Tancred said, "Come down, and let us in."

They went round to the front of the Pavilion; and Mr. Borrodaile heard the front door opened and their steps on the stairs. Then the door of his prison opened and the Prime Minister and Sir Tancred entered, followed by the three children. The Prime Minister sat down in a chair; and on the instant his breach of decorum was marked by the emphasis with which the English Raisuli drew forward chairs for Elsie and the Lady Noggs. The Prime Minister whose habitual mildness seemed to have been dissipated by the events of the morning, glared at him; but Tinker preserved, with apparently no difficulty in the world, the air of an innocent seraph. His trusty lieutenant was equally unembarrassed; but the Lady Noggs looked her most defiant.

Sir Tancred stood on the hearth-rug with his hands in his pockets, surveying the gathering with an impassive and judicial air, and said to the English Raisuli, "Now, if you'd explain."

The air of seraphic innocence appeared positively to thicken on his son's face as he said firmly, "Well, sir, it was the only thing to do."

"That I knew. It always is," said Sir Tancred patiently.

"We were out on the car, Elsie and I," Tinker went on. "And we found Lady Grandison and two boys, and there was some trouble. And we found she was going to sea; and that's a poor sort of thing to do, so we brought her here. She didn't seem to want to go back to Stonorill."

"I wouldn't go back to Stonorill!" broke in the Lady Noggs. "He's telling it all wrong. It was the Inquisition; and they were trying to lick me because I had run away with the kitten; and they'd have done it, if Tinker hadn't knocked them down and driven me away in the car. And I *was* running away to sea; and I should have got there and been a cabin-boy, and you'd never have seen me again, only Tinker and Elsie persuaded me not to go. And it was very good of them, for I'm sure that I really shouldn't have liked it at all; so you see it wasn't Tinker's fault at all — so there." And she paused for want of breath.

"Well, you see, it was no good Lady Grandison being here and doing nothing at all," said Tinker taking up the tale. "So I was Raisuli, and Elsie was my lieutenant; and Lady Grandison was Miss Perdicaris, our captive; and we had to ask a ransom for her because brigands do. Elsie went to Stonorill for the ransom; and Mr. Borrodaile captured her, and took our car and came here for Lady Grandison. He wanted to exchange prisoners; and of course the more prisoners there are to exchange the better, so he got locked up in the morning-room."

The Prime Minister's air had grown more and more bewildered. Along the tortuous paths of German Philosophy his mind could travel without a pause; but, confronted with this series of facts, it was entirely at a loss; and he said plaintively, "I don't understand a word of it."

"We will now proceed to unravel the tangle then," said Sir Tancred with a faint twinkle in his eye. "Who was the Inquisition, Lady Grandison?"

"They were two boys — horrid, fat boys," said the Lady Noggs. "I found them just going to question the kitten, they were going to stretch it and hurt it because it was a heretic; so I took it and bolted. And they had just caught me up, and were trying to lick me, when Tinker and Elsie came along in their car. And Tinker knocked the Inquisition down while I got into the car, and we drove away from them."

"This grows more and more complicated," said the Prime Minister.

"Oh, I think it's fairly plain," said Mr. Borrodaile. "The English Raisuli appears to have begun his acquaintance with Lady Felicia by rescuing her from two boys who were trying to beat her for preventing them torturing a kitten."

"That's it," said the Lady Noggs. "You do understand things sometimes, Billy."

"Your encomiums make me blush," said Mr. Borrodaile politely.

"Then Tinker saved you from some annoyance," said Sir Tancred.

"Well, I think they would have licked me in

the end," said the Lady Noggs frankly. "They were two to one you see, though I had got tight hold of one's hair, and bigger than me."

"Where did this happen?" said the Prime Minister.

"Out beyond Appleton," said the Lady Noggs.

"And what were you doing there?" said the Prime Minister.

"I was going to sea," said the Lady Noggs with a sudden accession of dignity. "I'm not going to stop in a place where people find fault with me all about nothing at all before everybody else. I wasn't ever going back to Stonorill. And I should have got to sea, only Tinker told me that it was a very rough life and no desert islands left."

"Evidently," said Sir Tancred. "we have to go yet further back. I can see looming in the distance behind all this some primal basic fact. Had you, or any of her pastors and masters any dispute with Lady Grandison?"

"I had only told her to stay in the nursery for the day, for making an apple-pie bed for one of my guests," said the Prime Minister stiffly.

"You told me before every one at breakfast," said the Lady Noggs bitterly.

"This puts a different complexion on the matter," said Sir Tancred. "It seems to me that had it not been for the intervention of my son, your niece would be leading a life on the ocean wave. I don't know of course if you proposed that career for her. It looks very much as if you owe her to him."

The Prime Minister looked at the English Raisuli with no great gratitude, and said, "It certainly looks like it, and so far I am grateful to him; but at the same time, his attempt to blackmail me was monstrous in one so young."

"Brigands have to have ransoms," said Tinker firmly.

"After all, Romance has its claims, though five hundred pounds in gold is rather a heavy one," said Mr. Borrodaile.

"I seem to have wandered into topsy-turvy-dom," said the Prime Minister wearily, and he rose. "At any rate I am much obliged to you, Sir Tancred, for releasing my secretary, and restoring my niece."

"And I must apologize for the length of my intrusion; but I can assure you it was involuntary," said Mr. Borrodaile.

"Not at all, not at all," said Sir Tancred. "But won't you have some tea, or a whisky and soda, or something after your drive through the heat ?"

"No, no; thank you," said the Prime Minister. "I must be at Stonorill for the afternoon post."

"Well, you must allow me to express my regret that your time should have been wasted like this," said Sir Tancred. And they drifted towards the door. The Lady Noggs, Tinker, and Elsie came down-stairs after them, and in hurried whispers fixed a place at which to meet on the morrow.

The Prime Minister, Mr. Borrodaile, and the Lady Noggs got into their car; and as the Prime Minister bent to start the engine, the Lady Noggs cried vindictively, "You kidnap uncle next time! I'll help!"

CHAPTER FIFTEEN

THE WEDDING GUEST

WHEN Mr. Beresford Caldecott cooled down after his visit to Stonorill, he regretted that in the outburst of fury, provoked by Mr. Borrodaile's use of the word bunco-steerer, he should have committed himself to make Violet an allowance. He had always been used to look back on those outbursts of fury with complacency; and that complacency had prevented him grasping the fact that if you apply the wild, free life of the far West to the naturally horny temperament of an English aristocrat, the result will, sooner or later, be discomfort to the possessor of that temperament. The thought of having to pay out two thousand a year, well as he could afford it, inspired into him a very acute discomfort. However, he was a man of his word; and he instructed his solicitor to make the needful settlement, to which he added what he hoped would prove a saving clause, the proviso that she should marry Mr. Borrodaile within the month.

Now and again he tried to cheer himself with the conviction that the young jackanapes, as he persisted in considering Mr. Borrodaile, had only been trifling with his niece's affections; and that the settlement would make no difference to his purpose of jilting her. The conviction was not very strong; and he got but little comfort out of it. This was as well; it saved him disappointment, for two days after he had signed the deed of settlement he received a letter of warm thanks from Violet, and the day after that a letter of warmer thanks from Mr. Borrodaile himself; a letter which drove him forthwith into his beautiful, sibilant Spanish. It was fortunate, indeed, for the land of his birth that his residence in South America had made Spanish the medium in which he expressed his deeper emotions.

Violet had been pleased indeed to receive the lawyer's letter informing her of her uncle's generous provision; but the proviso troubled her not a little. She could hardly go to Mr. Borrodaile and tell him about it. Fortunately, he himself relieved her of her embarrassment. She had been pondering the matter all day without finding any solution of the difficulty; and after dinner, she was walking up and down the lawn in front of the castle still wrestling with it, when he joined her.

"It is a great comfort to me to know that yours is not a wasteful disposition," he said, with his usual assured air.

"Why?" said Violet.

"Because," said Mr. Borrodaile coolly, "I am going to purchase a special marriage license, which is an expensive document; and I know you will not be able to bring yourself to let it be wasted. I am *sure* you won't allow it to be wasted."

"I suppose people who have that can get married in a month," said Violet, with a somewhat mocking reflection in her voice.

"You can get married in a month with banns," said Mr. Borrodaile. "With this you can get married in a week or less.

"No one can get married in a week," said Violet with conviction.

"They could with a little firmness," said Mr. Borrodaile.

Violet said nothing for a minute or two; then she began in a hasty fashion: "Talking about marriage I am in a somewhat awkward position.

I had a letter this morning, offering me an allowance of two thousand a year, if I get married within the month."

"Who to," said Mr. Borrodaile sharply.

"Well, the odd thing about it is, it's — it's to you."

"What! Your uncle has carried out his threat!" said Mr. Borrodaile.

It is needless to dwell on the events of the next few minutes; but Violet came into the castle with a very fine flush on her face, and Mr. Borrodaile's eyes were shining. He clung to his idea of a special license, and getting quietly married in London; but when the Prime Minister was informed of their good fortune he would not hear of this plan. Violet should properly have been married from Gradesleigh, but her uncle had not made this suggestion; and she said that she devoutly hoped that he would not make it. Therefore the Prime Minister proposed, or rather insisted, that she should be married from Stonorill; declaring that after her three years direction of the education of the Lady Noggs, he looked upon her as a member of his family. She was touched by the kindly offer and accepted it gratefully.

Accordingly, the wedding was fixed to take

place in three weeks; and Violet set about her preparations for it, declaring that three weeks was all too short a time for them. She was very busy with those preparations; and the Lady Noggs had the greater opportunities of enjoying the society of her two new young friends at Beauleigh.

She and Elsie showed an interest in the approaching marriage which seemed to Tinker quite out of proportion to the event, even though the Lady Noggs was to be a bridesmaid. He listened, however, to their discussions of it with exemplary patience. Then the Lady Noggs happened to let fall the statement that Mr. Beresford Caldecott was to be a wedding guest; that he had been called Tiger Jake in Arizona; and that he had described himself as a tough. At once Tinker was all interest. His wide, romantic reading enabled him to place Mr. Beresford Caldecott exactly; and he described the attributes of that bye-product of Western civilization, the tough, in terms which filled the Lady Noggs and Elsie with an admiring interest equal to his own.

At once, for them, the presence of Mr. Beresford Caldecott became by far the most important feature in the matter of the wedding ceremony, and all the other persons attending it were dwarfed into the most paltry insignificance by that interesting figure.

The discharge of her function of bridesmaid prevented the Lady Noggs pointing him out to them at the church itself; but when she came out of it, feeling considerably relieved from the strain of acting with the sedateness which her official position had demanded, she hurried to their motor-car in which they were already awaiting her, and watched with them the guests coming through the lych-gate to their carriages. At last she pointed out a dapper little man, with a very red face and a very shiny top hat, and said: "There he is. That's Tiger Jake."

Her two young companions scarcely believed their eyes; and, indeed, Mr. Beresford Calde-cott did not at all correspond with the figure of the desperado their imaginations had set up for them.

Tinker sighed, and said with some bitterness: "Ah, well, it isn't what a man looks like, of course, but what he does."

"I dare say when he begins to talk to us, he'll seem quite different," said Elsie.

Their motor-car followed the carriage which carried him to the castle. Its occupants followed him closely up the steps into the hall.

Mr. Beresford Caldecott had come to enjoy himself. His generosity had made the ceremony possible, and he was not on that account, going to let it be too pleasant, if any effort of his could prevent it. He was looking forward, indeed, to a regular field-day, and hoped to get in at least half a dozen bitter quarrels before the evening.

His first act on entering the great hall, where the reception was being held, was to make his way to the bride and bridegroom, who were receiving the congratulations of their friends. He greeted Violet with some curtness, and wished her happiness in accents of sepulchral gloom, calculated to demonstrate the hopelessness of the wish; then he made his way to the bridegroom who stood a few paces off. Mr. Borrodaile greeted him with as much of the warmth due to a benefactor, as he could command by an earnest effort.

"Ha! you're married now," said Mr. Beresford Caldecott, gloating over him with infinite malevolence.

"I am indeed," said Mr. Borrodaile cheerfully.

"Yes, you're cock-a-hoop about it now; but you wait — you wait," growled Mr. Beresford Caldecott.

"Well, sir, I shall have leisure to wait," said Mr. Borrodaile with unimpaired cheerfulness.

"You'll live to regret it; mark my words. I know the Caldecott temper."

"As the head of the family it has doubtless been brought to your notice," said Mr. Borrodaile politely.

Mr. Beresford Caldecott looked at him suspiciously, and said, "I do; I know it; none better; and if you want my opinion I don't mind telling you that I am sure you will live to be sorry — "

"How do you do, Mr. Caldecott?" broke in the Lady Noggs. "I am so glad you've come. I was afraid you wouldn't care enough about weddings; so was Tinker: but let me introduce you, Tiger Jake — Miss Elsie Brand — Mr. Hildebrand Anne Beauleigh." She shook him warmly by the hand, a limp and irresponsive hand, in the heartiest good-fellowship.

Mr. Beresford Caldecott stared at her somewhat uncertainly. In her bridesmaid's frock she was a radiant vision indeed; but it was a vision which by no means gladdened his heart. Indeed, it somewhat dashed the joy of battle he was beginning to feel; for he entertained a clear and uncomfortable remembrance of his earlier meeting with her. Mr. Borrodaile took advantage of the diversion to withdraw with swift discreetness to

Violet's side. Mr. Beresford Caldecott found himself being shaken warmly by the hand by a little girl and a small boy, who regarded him with admiring, almost reverential eyes.

"We've got a nice, long afternoon before us," said the Lady Noggs. "You'll be able to tell us lots about Arizona, and shooting people in saloons."

Mr. Beresford Caldecott cast a helpless, appealing glance round the hall, and muttered a few words under his breath. They sounded Spanish.

"Perhaps he'd like a drink first. They do," said Tinker.

At once the Lady Noggs became all hospitality. She took the unresisting wedding guest by the hand, led him to a table, and pressed refreshment upon him. She offered him the innocuous drinks his soul abhorred — hock-cup, claret-cup, champagne-cup, and cider-cup. He refused them all with great shortness, and was turning away from the table when Sir Hildebrand Wyse came up to them and greeted her. She shook hands with him, crying with joyful pride, "Oh, let me introduce you, Tiger Jake — Sir Hildebrand Wyse. He was a tough in Arizona, and used to shoot people in saloons."

Mr. Beresford Caldecott turned sharply to the table, and said in the husky voice of deep, restrained emotion, "Whisky! Whisky! Give me the bottle!"

The footman gave him the bottle; and, in spite of his training and experience, opened his eyes at the quantity Mr. Beresford Caldecott poured into the tumbler. He added to it a complimentary dash of water with a trembling hand, and turned to hear the Lady Noggs saying: " His name is Mr. Beresford Caldecott in England; but that's what they called him in Arizona. He shot people in saloons. Tinker says they do. "

Mr. Beresford Caldecott glared at his new acquaintance, and looked as if, had they been in Arizona, he would have shot him.

Sir Hildebrand Wyse bowed, and said with a somewhat embarrassed air: "Pleased to meet you. "

Mr. Beresford Caldecott produced an unintelligible but guttural sound from very low down in his throat, and his eyes rolled painfully. Sir Hildebrand Wyse moved hastily to the next group.

Mr. Beresford Caldecott took a feverish gulp at his whisky; then Tinker said, "There's hardly any water in it at all. Isn't it splendid to be able to drink it like that! — if you must drink whisky."

The three children watched him drink with immense admiration. When he set the glass down Tinker said, "We should be very much obliged if you'd tell us about the first man you shot."

"We should, awfully," said Elsie.

"Don't you think we ought to introduce him to some more people first?" said the Lady Noggs, whose sense of hospitality had been fully aroused. "He's a guest, you know; and I don't think we ought to keep him to ourselves altogether. Toughs are so rare in England; and there must be lots of people here who'd like to know Tiger — "

Mr. Beresford Caldecott's dash for freedom cut her short. He went with marked haste through the serried throng of guests, across the room, to the duchess.

"I'm glad to see you've come, Beresford," she said. "I was afraid you wouldn't. Those children seem to have taken a great fancy to you. I've been watching you and them. You're coming out in a new light. I've thought that a good deal of that temper of yours was put on; and I am beginning to see I was right. It was amiable of you to secure the happiness of these two young people by that handsome allowance — quite like a Christmas story — the crusty but benevolent uncle, don't you know?"

Mr. Beresford Caldecott could scarcely restrain himself from English. He clenched his teeth, shut his lips tight, and breathed heavily through his nose.

"The money will be so useful to William in his career," the duchess continued. "And he will go far — very far — everybody says so. I suppose they'll come and stay with you at Gradesleigh after their honeymoon."

"They won't!" snapped Mr. Beresford Caldecott.

"You ought to come out of your shell," said the duchess graciously. "You ought to go about more and meet more people."

"You mind your own business, Elizabeth! And I'll mind mine!" said Mr. Beresford Caldecott, with ravening ferocity.

"I only spoke for your good," said the duchess tartly.

"Have you done with him, aunty?" the Lady Noggs broke in. "We want him to tell us all about Arizona, and shooting people in saloons."

"Take him!" said the duchess, and she turned her back on him.

Before the hapless Mr. Beresford Caldecott could escape, the Lady Noggs had him firmly by the hand, and was leading him away to an empty corner of the hall. They hemmed him into it; and the Lady Noggs said: "Tell us about the first man you shot."

"Was it in a saloon?" said Elsie.

Mr. Beresford Caldecott freed his hand violently, and plunged into the thickest part of the throng. He went through it something after the manner of a snow-plough, and people stared after him, and asked who he was.

The three children looked at one another blankly. "It looks as if he didn't want to tell us about it," said the Lady Noggs.

"It does," said Tinker.

"Those brave men are so modest. All the books say so," said Elsie.

"I think it's grumpiness," said the Lady Noggs. "I know Violet is ever so frightened of him."

"It's very tiresome," said Elsie.

"People who go to weddings ought to be more obliging," said the Lady Noggs.

"Well, it doesn't seem much good bothering about him. Let's go and talk to Borrodaile," said Tinker.

They joined the group round Mr. Borrodaile, and lingered there a while; but it was no use: they were drawn towards the central fascinating figure of the gathering by an invincible attraction. In spite of themselves they found themselves hovering about him; and try as he would he could not keep a thick enough section of the throng between him and them. They said nothing to him, but where he was they were; and their mere presence prevented him giving the rein to his natural disposition. He had meant to be very severe with the Prime Minister; but his mind was so full of his limpet-like attendants that the Prime Minister only found him distrait and preoccupied.

In the meantime the children had had time to grow sore at his reticence; and, at last, Tinker said thoughtfully: "I'm thinking about that hat of his — that new silk hat. You say he jumps on his hats."

The Lady Noggs nodded.

"I wonder if we could do anything," said Tinker. "If he jumped on that hat, he wouldn't be such a disappointment."

The faces of the Lady Noggs and Elsie brightened.

"But we shall have to wait till he's got his hat on," said the Lady Noggs.

"It seems to me he doesn't like being introduced to people. We might do it that way, working him up by introducing people to him," said Tinker. "You see if they really called him Tiger Jake, we'd better not do anything too plain, or there might be no end of a row; and that wouldn't do at all: you can't have rows at weddings, you know."

"Let's try introducing them," said the Lady Noggs.

In the course of the next ten minutes Mr. Beresford Caldecott was introduced to three men and two ladies as Tiger Jake of Arizona. He really did not know whether he hated most those who treated the introduction as an engaging jest of the Lady Noggs and laughed heartily, or those who eyed him with gathering affright; but he broke away from the group of new acquaintances, with which his little hostess had so thoughtfully provided him, and simmering very near boiling point escaped to a refreshment table.

At this moment the Lady Noggs perceived

Lord Grasthwaite, and cried: "Look, there is that horrid sneak, Lord Grasthwaite! I'll introduce him. If he does have a row with him no one'll mind much. "

"Come on," said Tinker.

Without knowing exactly what was happening to him, Lord Grasthwaite was conveyed by three active and voluble children to the table at which stood a little red-faced man, with a glass in his hand, surrounded by an atmosphere of whisky; and the Lady Noggs said, with crisp distinctness, "Let me introduce you, Tiger Jake — Lord Grasthwaite. He was called Tiger Jake in Arizona because he was a tough, and used to shoot people in saloons."

The timid minister recoiled in open-mouthed dismay, but managed to stammer, "D — d — de — lighted t — t — to m — m — meet you."

Mr. Beresford Caldecott turned on him a face of an exasperated fiend, and said thickly: "I wish there were saloons in England. I wish we were in a saloon. I'd delight you, you mutton-headed gaping idiot!"

Lord Grasthwaite gasped, and staggered hastily away.

Mr. Beresford Caldecott gulped down the rest of his whisky, and turned to berate the children.

For the first time in the afternoon, as it seemed to him, they were nowhere in sight.

There was a lull in the conversation and a general movement towards the door. The guests streamed out of it, gathered on the steps, or crossed the drive and grouped themselves on the lawn to see the departure of the bride and bridegroom.

Mr. Beresford Caldecott got his hat and went with them. He found the cooler open air grateful to his heated brow. The three children were standing on the lawn close to him. The bride and bridegroom came out of the door, flushed and smiling. The Lady Noggs tore herself from the vicinity of Mr. Beresford Caldecott, and ran across the drive to kiss Violet good-bye. The bride and bridegroom got into the carriage, and some one gave the Lady Noggs a shoe to throw after them. The carriage started amid a chorus of good wishes; and, by a skilful shot, the Lady Noggs struck Mr. Borrodaile a shrewd blow with the shoe. Then she ran down the steps, across the drive to Mr. Beresford Caldecott, and reached him just in time to hear Tinker saying to his father and stepmother: "Let me introduce you; Tiger Jake — Lady Beauleigh — Sir Tancred Beauleigh. They call him Tiger Jake in

Arizona, because he was a tough and shot people in saloons."

Mr. Beresford Caldecott jammed his hat down over his eyes, and strode away towards the line of carriages. At the end of ten strides his feelings were too much for him; he snatched his hat from his head, dashed it to the ground, leapt into the air, and came down on it with both feet. Then he gave it a vicious, parting kick, sprang into the nearest carriage, and cried, "The Station!"

Among the amazed, enquiring throng of his fellow guests, three happy children screamed with laughter.

THE END

THE McCLURE PRESS, NEW YORK

www.ingramcontent.com/pod-product-compliance
Lightning Source LLC
Chambersburg PA
CBHW022219010726
47493CB00002B/524